Twilight

ELIE WIESEL

Translated from the French by
Marion Wiesel

PENGUIN BOOKS

PENGUIN BOOKS

Published by the Penguin Group
Penguin Books Ltd, 80 Strand, London WC2R ORL, England
Penguin Group (USA) Inc., 375 Hudson Street, New York, New York 10014, USA
Penguin Group (Canada), 90 Eglinton Avenue East, Suite 700, Toronto, Ontario, Canada M4P 2Y3
(a division of Pearson Penguin Canada Inc.)
Penguin Ireland, 25 St Stephen's Green, Dublin 2, Ireland (a division of Penguin Books Ltd)
Penguin Group (Australia), 707 Collins Street, Melbourne, Victoria 3008, Australia
(a division of Pearson Australia Group Pty Ltd)
Penguin Books India Pvt Ltd, 11 Community Centre, Panchsheel Park, New Delhi – 110 017, India
Penguin Group (NZ), 67 Apollo Drive, Rosedale, Auckland 0632, New Zealand
(a division of Pearson New Zealand Ltd)
Penguin Books (South Africa) (Pty) Ltd, Block D, Rosebank Office Park,
181 Jan Smuts Avenue, Parktown North, Gauteng 2193, South Africa

Penguin Books Ltd, Registered Offices: 80 Strand, London WC2R ORL, England

www.penguin.com

First published in France, under the title *Le Crépuscule, au loin*,
by Editions Bernard Grasset & Fasquelle 1987
This English translation first published in the USA by Summit Books,
a division of Simon & Schuster, Inc., New York 1988
First published in Great Britain by Viking 1988
Published in Penguin Books 1991
Reissued in this edition 2013
001

Set in 11/13pt Dante MT Std
Typeset by Jouve (UK), Milton Keynes
Printed in Great Britain by Clays Ltd, St Ives plc

ISBN: 978-0-241-96367-8

www.greenpenguin.co.uk

Penguin Books is committed to a sustainable
future for our business, our readers and our planet.
This book is made from Forest Stewardship
Council™ certified paper.

For my sister, Bea,
in memoriam

'The world couldn't exist without madmen.'

Maimonides

'Never shall I forget that night, the first night in camp, which turned my life into long night, seven times cursed and seven times sealed. Never can I forget those flames that consumed my faith for ever. Never shall I forget that nocturnal silence which deprived me, for all eternity, of the desire to live.'

Elie Wiesel

I am going mad, Pedro. I feel it. I know it. I have plunged into madness as into the sea. And I am about to sink to its depths. Infinity cannot be challenged with impunity, and madness is infinite down to its fragments. As is death. As is God. Cry for help? Here, everybody cries for help. Our voices drown, resurface, merge, and dissolve while on the outside life goes on. What am I to do, Pedro? To whom shall I turn for a little light, a little warmth? Madness is lying in wait for me and I am alone.

As a boy, Raphael feared madness but was drawn to madmen. In his hometown, deep in the Carpathian Mountains, there was an asylum. That was where he spent his Shabbat afternoons. Each week he would arrive bearing fruit and sweets. And each week he would find himself looking for a certain old man, an old man with veiled eyes. Raphael remembered that on his very first visit the old man had smiled at him gently, and that he had been inexplicably moved.

'What is your name?' the old man had asked as the boy was leaving.

'Raphael, Raphael Lipkin,' he had answered timidly.

'Will you come see me again, Raphael?'

'Yes, sir. I'll come again.'

'Thank you, my boy. You deserve a blessing. Would you like me to bless you?'

'Yes, sir, I would.'

But the old man had retreated into his dreams. Emerging briefly he said, 'Next time.'

'Will you still be here?'

'Oh, yes.' The old man's voice was sad, ironic. 'I'll be here even when I'm no longer here.'

Raphael did not understand. But how could he? The old man was mad, and madmen put little store in being understood. Madmen can say anything, do or undo anything, without ever having to explain. Madmen are free, totally free. Perhaps that's why Raphael found the old man appealing.

'Be careful,' warned a young doctor. 'This man is dangerous.'

'But, Doctor, he seems so gentle.'

'That's why he's dangerous.'

Raphael refused to believe him. Still, he must have believed him a little, enough for the patient to notice. The following Shabbat the old man greeted him, a mischievous look on his still-handsome face.

'So, that's how it is. You're hiding things from me.'

'Oh, no, sir. I'm not hiding anything.'

'Yes, you are! I know it! They warned you against me.'

'Nobody . . .'

'Hush, my boy. You must never lie to a madman. We see right through you.'

'I won't lie to you ever again.'

'Good. Now let's examine the situation: They told you I'm dangerous . . . right?'

'That's what they said. But . . .'

'But you don't believe it? Well, you'd better believe it. I order you to. For your own good. Madmen can be dangerous, and I more than the others: I see farther, higher than any of them. They are dangerous when they're present. I am dangerous even when I'm absent. That's why I can go on protecting you even after I'm gone. Of course, to be protected by madness can also be dangerous.'

'I don't understand,' said Raphael.

'Come, my boy. Let's get some air.'

The old man led Raphael to a secluded bench at the outer edge of the garden.

'Who sent you?' asked the old man.

'My . . . my parents.'

'And who sent them?'

'I don't know, sir.'

For a moment, the old man lost his patience: 'You don't know, you don't know . . . One day you will have to know . . . Fortunately, that day I'll be there to guide you.'

'Guide me?' wondered Raphael. 'Where?'

'Toward knowledge, my boy. Toward knowledge.'

Then, for no apparent reason, he began to laugh.

'You will follow me, won't you?'

'Yes,' Raphael heard himself say. 'I will follow you.'

Thus went their weekly visits: the patient spoke and Raphael listened. The more he listened, the less he understood. The old man spoke of God and His attributes, and of the ten *Sephirot*, which collectively symbolize the king's crown and majestic power. He described an invisible palace surrounded by fiery walls where the Creator of the world awaits the *Shekhina* to restore his Creation to the origins of innocence. And the eagle's nest where a lone, melancholy Messiah prays for time to accelerate its rhythm, for words to open themselves to the Word . . .

'The place I want to show you is farther still,' said the old man. 'Promise to follow me always.'

'Always,' vowed Raphael, entranced.

'If ever you're afraid to go forward,' said the madman, 'hold onto me tightly. That way you won't fall. True, the road is treacherous. Satan is full of tricks. Sometimes he appears in the guise of a vicious black dog, a monster who spits fire. But bear in mind that he fears courage, so don't ever close your eyes, my boy. If you wish to accompany me, you must promise to keep your eyes open. Otherwise the black dog will attack you and all will be lost. Remember: a madman is someone whose eyes are always open.'

Raphael opened his eyes but saw no dog. Then he closed his eyes and saw the old man laughing, laughing without a sound.

'I don't understand,' said Raphael.

'You cannot understand,' said the old man. 'You *must* not understand. If you understood, you would already be mad.'

In his dimly lit room at the Mountain Clinic, Raphael remembers the old man of his childhood, his veiled eyes. And he thinks he finally understands his warning.

I am going mad, Pedro. Now I am sure. There are times when I think the old man and I are one. Still, after the storm comes the calm. I vacillate between the two extremes and all the time I see the gaping mouth of the vicious black dog, everywhere I see the bottom of the abyss. I am afraid and yet I yearn to hurl myself into it. I move forward and backward at the same time, with the same step, the same purpose. I speak when I am silent, I am silent when I shout. I hear the doctor telling me: 'Be careful, madmen are dangerous. You, Raphael Lipkin, are dangerous.'

Me, dangerous? Why would I be dangerous? Because I know the truth? But I don't. Because I seek it? What a joke! It eludes me, as reason eludes me.

Outside, a mild breeze is blowing toward the mountain, sweeping me back to my childhood. On the way, it is you I find. You, Pedro, my friend, the source of my strength and of my anguish.

It is still early but the clinic is asleep. Down below, the village too is asleep. As for me, I am afraid of sleep. An old man is waiting for me in my dreams; I know and I don't know, I no longer know, who he is.

In my dreams I seek someone with the courage to denounce reality's apparent order. I find the old madman who questions all my certainties.

Sky slides over roof, stone over stone, living over dead. Thought slides over dream, dream over memory, prayer over the tears of the dying.

Look, Pedro. I am moving closer to the wall. One more step, one more word, and I'll be on the other side.

And then I will think differently, express myself in another mode, react in untried ways. I will take leave of my body, reach for another self, integrate it into a distant time, and wrap it in garb that was never mine.

Farewell, Raphael. Farewell, Pedro.

How did he get to this point? Raphael wonders. Madness has its own design, its own dynamic. To dismantle it, he would have to confront it from the outside, so to speak. Raphael cannot. How could he? The madness is already inside him.

He leaves his bed, walks to the window overlooking the garden, opens it. Through the trees he sees the stars and a thousand shadows dancing. Raphael plays at identifying them. He beckons to them, they respond. What if he were to join them? If he jumped from his third-floor window all of the stars and shadows – and even the old man – would rush to greet him. 'To fall very low, one must first rise very high,' the old man had said. So go ahead, Raphael, jump! Follow the light God has hidden in the darkness. Go away and never come back. What matters is to laugh at death so as never to fear it again. And then? And then nothing, you fool. The earth will keep turning around the black sun, the black sun of madmen.

And then, when time runs out, we shall see the evil dawn of the suicides.

Raphael leaves the window and goes over to the table, picks up a book and puts it down. He clenches and unclenches his fist, as if to gauge the power of his elusive will, wondering how much he has in common with the patients in the hospital garden. They seem like broken puppets, oblivious of the world's joys and miseries. He must decide: to listen or never listen again, to the song of blind birds and the laughter of old men in mourning.

The muffled sound of voices drifts in from the director's residence. He and his guests must be enjoying themselves. A disquieting thought: Is the enemy there, among them, celebrating his victory over Pedro and me? I should have accepted the invitation, thinks Raphael: my midnight caller, my nemesis, may well be there.

Dr Benedictus, the clinic's director, was giving a dinner party in honor of a psychiatrist who publishes erotic novels under a pseudonym. Raphael is annoyed. Why had he given the tired excuse of a sudden migraine? Why hadn't he gone? True, he wasn't hungry. He hasn't been hungry in weeks. Not since that first anonymous phone call denouncing Pedro. Suddenly, an even more disquieting thought: Pedro is there among the guests. An older, unfamiliar Pedro. Though surely not without the pipe he'd always carried with him. What if I've come to this wretched place for the sole purpose of meeting Pedro in the director's library? God, what have I done? After all these years of searching, he could be there, just a few steps away . . . Wait a minute, Raphael. Pedro is dead, or at best, wasting in a Soviet prison . . . Who knows? Maybe this is my chance to resolve the mystery that weighs on me like a curse.

Like a condemned man, Raphael examines the space around him: the walls, the ceiling, the books strewn all over the floor –

and then those dead people holding up the holy scrolls of the Torah. What are *they* doing here? If they stay, he is sure to wind up with one of those colossal headaches . . . Soon his migraine is no longer a pretense. It whips his temples, roars in his brain, trying to burst its walls . . . Fine, he'll have to lie down, behave as if the dead were not there, as if Pedro were not in danger, as if he were in some hotel in Calcutta or Madras rather than at the Mountain Clinic. He needs to focus on a distant object, perhaps the shiny leaf which has finally come to rest on his windowsill . . . Above all, he must not think of the anonymous calls, the innuendos, the aspersions cast on Pedro's character . . .

The tiles of his room are blue and white. Blank squares alternate with pictures: a bird hovers in a peaceful sky, a little girl in a blue dress is chasing it. Ezra, Raphael thinks, my brother Ezra also loved birds. The pictures are soothing. Everything here is calculated to serve the patient. All is familiar yet oddly troubling: one feels at home while knowing that one is not.

Tell me, Pedro, whose body is this? Surely it's not mine . . . The black dog is moaning within me. The orphan is crying at the cemetery. The wolf is howling in the forest. Go on, you wanderer in time, go on: speak. I am listening.

'Can you hear me?' asks the old man with the veiled eyes. 'You have nothing to fear. I shall save you.'

And strange as it may seem, he did.

Rovidok: a pretty town in Galicia, a colorful town. Though its inhabitants were from different religious and ethnic backgrounds, it had endured the centuries with unusual grace. Rarely affected by external events other than the occasional war or epidemic, Jews and Christians had coexisted harmoniously.

A harmony barely disrupted by the anti-Semitic incidents that predictably occurred at Easter and Christmas. Ever since Christianity had driven Israel into exile, Christians who were not necessarily followers of Christ had considered it their duty to persecute Jews in the name of love and mercy. That's how it was, and nothing could be done about it. The Jews had learned to accept these eruptions of hatred as others accept inclement weather. Not so terrible, they said. Two days and two nights a year. Not so terrible. All one had to do was stay home.

'Why can't we go outside?' asked Raphael, who was seven.

'It's better not to,' replied his father.

'Why is it better?'

'It's safer.'

'Why is it safer?'

'It's dangerous outside.'

'Why is it dangerous?'

'Our enemies are there.'

'Our enemies? Who are they?'

'Those who hate Jews.'

Raphael's eyes opened wide. 'Why do they hate us? What did we do to them? What did we steal from them?'

His father smiled. 'I cannot explain it to you, my son. You are too young. One day you will understand.'

'If I'm old enough to be hated, I'm old enough to understand,' said Raphael solemnly.

'Some things cannot be explained, Raphael. Hatred is one of them. Madness is another. And one often leads to the other.'

Raphael still had many questions. He asked them in order to hear his father speak. He loved to hear him speak. That was his profession, his calling. Aharon Lipkin spent his life with children. He taught them to read and write, to sing, to dream, to grow up and be good Jews. He was tall and bushy-haired. His pupils feared him. Raphael thought that was funny. He

knew better: his father was the gentlest man on earth. So gentle that Raphael's mother often chided her husband:

'A man must know how to inspire respect.'

'Are you implying that I don't?'

'You know what I mean.'

He knew, and so did Raphael. Rivka still had not accepted the fact that Ezra and Yoel no longer lived at home. They had left, not to study in a yeshiva, which would have gratified Aharon, but to learn a trade. One had gone to Lodz, the other to Lvov.

'God is Almighty,' said Aharon. 'And He is everywhere.'

'I never denied that. But it is not God our sons went looking for in Lvov and Lodz. Tell me, what if they left to get away from God?'

Aharon bowed his head until it almost rested on the ancient book in front of him.

'Our sons are good and faithful. I trust them.'

'And who says I don't? All I say is, I don't trust the people they'll meet in Lodz and Lvov.'

It was the ongoing discussion of couples who love their children and can't bear to see them leave. In this particular case, the fear was compounded because Raphael's third brother, Hayim, often spoke of going to Palestine. 'If you want to kill me, go right ahead,' his mother would say. 'What's more, such behavior could spoil Ruth's engagement to Mendel. And with such a family, what chance would Esther ever have of finding a husband?'

Rivka Lipkin then turned to her youngest son:

'Thank God you're here, my Raphael,' she said. 'I know you won't make us worry. I won't have sleepless nights on your account.'

She was wrong.

One morning, the town learned the chilling news: two

cases of typhoid fever had been diagnosed at the hospital. At once, fear silenced all talk of the blizzard that had swept over the region; or of the police who were terrorizing the local merchants. People spoke only of the plague that crept through the streets, cunning and invisible. An eerie mood hung over the town: its inhabitants lowered their voices for fear of being noticed, for fear of attracting the plague's attention. They saw it as a monstrous creature, stronger, more agile, than any man. And as merciless as the Angel of Death. In markets and squares, churches and synagogues, there were those who discussed what measures to take, and those who were content to pray. From time to time news filtered down: the doctor had been seen entering so and so's house. May God help them, they would say, while thinking, May God help us all.

No doubt remained: only a divine intervention could halt the epidemic whose ravages multiplied with dizzying speed. In a few weeks the whole town had fallen prey to the scourge. Schools were closed, public meetings canceled. Few were the families that had not been struck.

The hospital was overcrowded: patients were lying on stretchers in the hallways. Emergency measures were in effect. New cases were directed to the asylum, whose second floor had been requisitioned for quarantine patients. And that is where, though it was not Shabbat, Raphael once again met his old friend the madman.

The disease caught up with Raphael one evening as he was watching his father studying a text on Purim, which was drawing near. His mother was pouring streams of hot tea. 'It's good for you' she kept saying. Ruth, the bride-to-be, was mending a shirt. Esther was indulging in her favorite pastime, looking through boxes of old family photographs. Hayim, the Zionist, had gone on an errand.

'I'm hot,' said Raphael. Then: 'I'm cold.'

'I knew you'd catch pneumonia,' said his mother. 'I begged you to button your overcoat, didn't I? Nobody ever listens to me.'

A few minutes later, Raphael complained of a headache and was sent to bed with a hot brick. By then, everybody knew what was happening but nobody dared say so. The entire family stayed at his bedside all night. He was delirious, burning with fever, and in pain, terrible pain. His throat, his chest, every particle of his flesh, every cell of his body was on fire. His mother applied cold compresses, massaged his aching limbs. But whatever was tormenting him refused to give in. His sister Esther even placed an amulet covered with mystical inscriptions under his pillow. But it didn't help. By morning the truth had to be faced: Raphael had come down with typhus.

If any shred of doubt remained, the doctor dispelled it at once. His order was curt: 'To the hospital!' He made no attempt to soften the blow.

'Never,' said Raphael's mother defiantly. 'Do you hear me? Never. Never shall I permit my son to be taken from me.'

Controlling his impatience, the doctor replied:

'I understand your distress, Mrs Lipkin. But you, too, must understand: your son has typhus, he requires constant care.'

'I know that,' said Rivka. 'I'll take care of him day and night. Nobody will do it better than I.'

Again the doctor restrained himself.

'Mrs Lipkin, I do not doubt your devotion, but you are not qualified to nurse this kind of patient. Believe me, your son must not, *cannot* stay at home.'

In the ensuing hush, the only sound to be heard was Raphael's labored breathing in the next room. His brother and sisters stared at the floor. His father did not seem anxious to speak either.

'You are not only a physician but also a Jew,' said the mother, raising her voice. 'What kind of Jew are you? Your heart, could it be made of stone? Don't you know it's a mother's place to be with her sick child?'

Wearily the doctor turned to Aharon: 'Please, Mr Lipkin, reason with her. You are an intelligent man, an educated man. Explain to your wife that if she cares about your son, if she wishes to see him recover, we must take him to the hospital immediately. Not tomorrow, not this afternoon, but at once. Because it's not . . .' He pulled out a handkerchief, mopped his brow, and continued:

'It's not just he, it's all of you. One doesn't play with typhus. I know of cases where entire families have been wiped out. I warn you, every minute counts. Not only for the boy but for all of you. You must let me help you!'

For the first time since his wedding day, Aharon made a decision without consulting his wife.

'I thank you for what you are doing for us, Doctor. Raphael will go to the hospital.'

Accepting her defeat, Rivka muttered something about getting her son dressed.

'No need,' said the doctor. 'Just cover him with warm blankets, that will do. I'll carry him to my sled.'

The entire family followed Raphael outside. Esther wept.

'How soon may I visit him?' asked the mother.

'Not for a few days. He will be isolated. In quarantine.'

'But . . .'

'Trust me. I'll keep you informed.'

An hour later, a woman wrapped in a black shawl could be seen in front of the asylum, staring up at the second-floor windows. At nightfall she went home, but returned the next morning. The freezing cold did not deter her. Once in a while, she would summon her courage, walk up to the doctor as he came or went, and ask, shyly but insistently:

'How is he? Does he have fever? Is he eating? Does he know that his father recites psalms for him from morning till night? And that he fasts on Mondays and Thursdays? Does he know that Rabbi Pinhas-the-Great sends him his blessing?'

Moved by her devotion, the doctor showed unusual patience. He answered, explained, reassured, and tried time and again to convince her not to keep vigil, not to risk her own health – in a word, to go home.

'I promise you, Mrs Lipkin, that the moment I have news . . . Trust me . . . I'm doing all I can . . . By staying here like this, you are not helping him . . . You'll get sick . . . When he really needs his mother, she, too, will be in the hospital . . .'

It was useless. She listened politely, never contradicting him. But the following day, there she was again, standing watch in her customary place opposite the dismal structure.

In the meantime, the shadow of death had spread over the whole town. Thirty-two casualties were recorded in one week. Faced with such suffering, Rabbi Pinhas-the-Great convened a meeting of his leading disciples. At that meeting it was decided to make use of an ancient remedy, that of marrying two orphans at the cemetery. There was no dearth of candidates. The choice fell on Zelig-the-Lame, a descendant of poor but devout people, and Hannah-Leah, nicknamed 'the dancer' as the unfortunate girl could neither walk straight nor think straight nor see straight; everything about her was deformed.

Zelig and Hannah-Leah were summoned to the rabbi, who offered to marry them and proposed as wedding gifts a hut near the river, two bags of flour, a dozen hens, and enough firewood to last three years. A few days later the wedding took place in the presence of the entire community. The cemetery became a place for singing, dancing, and drinking. It was as if the people of Rovidok were beseeching their dead to understand the living, not to begrudge them their appetite for life, not to punish them – in short, to put an end to the plague that was decimating the town.

The rabbi stopped at the grave of his illustrious grandfather, Rabbi Yaakov of Rovidok, author of a brilliant commentary on the Zohar, a man whose reputation as a miracle worker had reached far beyond Galicia's borders.

'Grandfather,' prayed the rabbi, 'you who have access to the Celestial Tribunal, I beg of you to plead on our behalf. Our despair is great, our grief infinite. Our men are weary of digging graves. Our women have run out of tears. God must intervene, Grandfather, He must.'

Throughout the cemetery, descendants of wise men sought help from their forebears. And, if one is to believe the official chronicler of Rovidok, the scourge ended one week later. 'Our ancestors have saved us, praise God,' stated the chronicler with conviction.

As for Raphael, he owed his salvation to someone else.

It happened . . . No, he does not know when it happened. Was it night? Was it dawn? He was too ill to care. The light inside the darkness eluded him. In his delirium, he saw himself climb hills and venture into the forest where elves and demons taunted him, trying to tear off his clothes, to lead him astray. He had a vision of himself as sad but happy, vulnerable but invincible, all at the same time. He saw himself as handsome but ugly, serene but restless, alive but dead. There he was in his room, sliding down an icy river, looking on as flames rose, from his chest. He was shouting, 'Help, help!' And a voice answered, 'Everything will be all right, my boy. You'll see, everything will be all right.' The voice was slightly hoarse, familiar.

'You? What are you doing in my room? What are you doing in my dream?'

The old man with the veiled eyes was smiling.

'Have you forgotten, my boy? I live here.'

'Yes, I had forgotten,' answered Raphael. 'I've forgotten so many things.'

'Remember, this is my home. I found out that you were here, so I came down right away.'

At that moment Raphael felt a great calm settle over him. No more moaning, no more death rattles. He heard only the soothing voice of his mad friend. What about the others? he wondered. What happened to the others on his floor? Could they all have died? Recovered? Could *I* be dead? And my friend too? Raphael opened his eyes, closed them, opened them again. He saw the old man watching him.

'Are you afraid, my boy?'

'Yes . . . no . . . a little.'

'What are you afraid of? Death?'

'Yes, I am afraid of death.'

'Don't be. Death is more afraid than you are. Didn't you know? Death is afraid . . . to die.'

Raphael smiled. He remembered a song from Passover night, a children's song about the chain of evil. At the end, the Angel of Death, having slaughtered the slaughterer, is himself slaughtered by the Holy One, blessed be He.

'You're smiling,' said the old man. 'A good sign. You're no longer afraid.'

Raphael shook his head. 'Oh, no, I'm still afraid.'

The old man came to sit on the boy's bed.

'If you're afraid to die, let me reassure you. You won't die. Not here. Not now. Not of this particular illness. You may ask: How do I know? Am I a prophet? Not at all. The prophets are locked up in the pavilion next door. I know that you will not die because I have just concluded my negotiations with heaven: I shall die in your place. And not only in yours. I shall die in place of all the doomed souls in this town. No, it was not easy. Satan confronted me before the Celestial Tribunal, determined to defeat my plan. As always, he argued in the name of reason and justice, whereas I pleaded in the name of passion, therefore of compassion. I couldn't bear it anymore, seeing all those widows and orphans, all that pain. I couldn't bear it anymore listening to the screams of children writhing in Death's twisted claws. How could I watch a whole town drown in despair? Fortunately, our ancestors, jolted from their long sleep, lent me their support. I carried the day. My terms were accepted. I myself heard the president of the Tribunal announce its verdict in a voice that filled the universe . . . That's it, the whole story, so stop being afraid. You'll live! Rovidok will breathe again! The enemy has been disarmed, the scourge has been routed. The living will go on living.'

As the old man spoke, Raphael was overcome by a sense of well-being, of serenity. Gone were the pains in his chest, the needles pricking him, the chills. He saw himself under the apple tree in his grandfather's orchard. The day was mild. In the distance, horses were neighing. A fragrant breeze carried sounds of sheeps' bells and shepherds' flutes from the hills.

Suddenly he had a terrible thought:

'But if you die, it means I'll never see you again!'

'It does mean something, but not that,' said the old man. 'I'll be dead, but you'll go on seeing me.'

'Then nothing will change?'

'Something will. My eyes. Look at them. Look at them closely.'

Raphael did as he was told. Leaning forward, he stared into the old man's eyes and saw for the first time that, though veiled, they reflected a distant, mysterious light.

'Don't tell anybody,' said the old man. 'Don't reveal to anyone that our town owes its survival to a madman, to me.'

He rose, lightly touched the patient's forehead, and was gone.

A few hours later – or was it days – Raphael, waking, heard the doctor whispering to a colleague, 'His fever is down; the worst is over.'

Within moments, the doctor was in the street, reassuring the boy's mother. 'He'll live, your son will live! You can go home now.'

'Are you sure, Doctor? Are you absolutely sure?'

'Mrs Lipkin, he will live.'

'Praise God, and may He bless you, Doctor.'

Whereupon she resumed her vigil in front of the hospital. The doctor looked at her in disbelief.

'Go home, Mrs Lipkin. There is no more reason for you to stay out here in the cold.'

'I must see him. Then I'll go home.'

'You cannot go inside. It's forbidden. There is still a danger of contagion.'

'I am not leaving until I have seen him.'

Three nights later, she thought she saw Raphael waving to her from the window. He seemed to be leaning against the doctor. Covering her mouth to stifle the cry she had been holding back so long, she silently turned and went home to share the news.

'Praise God,' she murmured. And fainted.

I am convinced, Pedro, that I am going mad. I may even be mad already. Is this me I glimpse in the mirror? Is this me speaking to you, speaking to myself? Is this me writing to you? Why is my hand trembling? Why do I feel that I'm awake even when I sleep? Why do I feel as if another were sleeping inside me? In my dream, I see two boys running toward the sea, one chasing the other, and I don't know whether I am the one or the other, or the spectator watching them, or the drowning man crying for help. Is this what madness is like?

You must admit, it is not normal, this need to cry out against sound and light – against the sound of light. The need to scream out after silently inveighing against the violence of twilight which refuses to heed the prayer of the stars. I'm telling you, it's not normal, my need to run from this room, this place, this existence, and to speak to the trees, the flowers, the rivers, to listen to them too. For they can express themselves, did you know that? They have their own language. They speak to our ears, even to our lips, our fingers. In springtime everything sings: the branches, the blossoms, the leaves. Every blade of grass sings in its own way, said the great Hasidic storyteller Rabbi Nahman of Bratslav.

Even the clouds can go mad. When they do, their song becomes dangerous. Never mind, I love it anyway. I will listen to it until it becomes a part of me. I will be a tree in the forest, a flower among the thorns. I will die with the sun, I will rise with the dawn. I will follow in the footsteps of a mad old man who died more than once. I will rediscover his madness, I will return to its source.

Don't leave me, Pedro.

September 1, 1939. The day war broke out in Poland. A day that had started badly for Raphael. He was late. Late for services, late for breakfast, late for school. He had slept poorly and woke feeling uneasy. For the rest of the day nothing went right. He had recited his prayers without concentration, he had eaten without appetite. The milk at breakfast was sour. His sister teased him even before he could say good morning. And worst of all, he spent hours trying to reconcile a single passage in the Babylonian and Palestinian texts of the Talmud. Seated around the long table in the dining room, the schoolboys were acting up in the teacher's absence. Come to think of it, where was his father? He who always started his classes on time was late. When he finally appeared, he seemed shaken.

'It's war,' he said. 'Boys, go home at once!'

The family gathered in the kitchen. Aharon and Rivka sat down at the table, the children remained standing.

'What are we going to do?' asked Ruth. 'We can't postpone the wedding!'

'Don't worry,' said Aharon.

'We'll see,' said Rivka, her hands looking abandoned in her lap. She let her thoughts stray:

'There will be a general mobilization, Ruth. Your Mendel will be called up. And then . . .'

Before she finished her sentence, Ruth had begun to cry. Aharon announced:

'I will cable your brothers. I want them home. In times like these, a family belongs together.'

'Thank God they're too young to be called up,' said Rivka.

They discussed war as they would any natural disaster. Eventually it would pass. It never occurred to them that this war might be bloodier, more lethal, than all others. They should have known better: Hitler had warned them in speech after speech. Tragically, they, and the rest of their community, believed their friends' assurances more than their enemies' threats.

The Germans entered the town on the second day of Rosh Hashanah. At first, the Polish army, though ill-equipped, put up a brave defense. But it was hopeless. By the time the fighting ended, the motorized *Wehrmacht* units had blocked off the major arteries, while the infantry had occupied the municipal offices. A lightning operation had taken place as in a void. There was not a passerby in the street. Not a store open. Few of the townspeople ventured outside, except for some Jews who stubbornly went to their synagogues. This New Year, the prayers of the faithful were more fervent than ever before.

Raphael and his family went to services at the House of Study of Rabbi Pinhas-the-Great. When the rabbi reached the litany describing the Day of Awe as the day when the Celestial Tribunal decides the fate of all beings – who shall live and who shall die; who shall perish by the sword, who by hunger, and who by fire – the entire community broke into sobs. The congregation sobbed so hard it was inconceivable that God could remain deaf. Then, just before the end of services, a man came running with the news: the Germans had arrived!

All eyes were on the rabbi, no one said a word. He turned to his flock, covered his head with his *tallit,* and declared solemnly, 'Whoever wishes to go home now, let him go and not wait till the end of the service. Whoever decides to stay, let him stay. May God grant all our prayers. One of my prayers is addressed to you: *Cling to hope.*'

A few men and women left, their heads bowed.

Raphael and his family stayed to the end. They squeezed the rabbi's hand, wished him a good year, and left. They took backstreets, kept close to the walls, and did not utter a word until they were back in their house. In the safety of her kitchen, Rivka broke down.

'God in Heaven,' she sobbed, 'save my children and yours. God in Heaven, God in Heaven, listen to a Jewish mother's prayer: stretch out your arm and shield us.'

Then she collected herself and set the table. Aharon recited the *Kiddush,* blessed the wine and bread, tried to sing a Hasidic melody but stopped midway. His eldest daughter was staring at him.

'I'm thinking of my Mendel,' said Ruth.

'And what about your brothers? Where are they? Why haven't they come home? Why aren't they here with us?'

'We must not give up hope,' said Aharon. 'That is the rabbi's order. That is God's will. The Germans may not be as cruel as people say.'

'We'll see,' said Rivka.

The Germans issued a proclamation directing all residents to gather in the main square, in front of the town hall, the following Saturday, at ten in the morning.

That day, the Jews proceeded toward the designated place in silence. As did the Poles. No one knew what to expect. So far, the occupying army had refrained from abusing its power. One by one the shops, including the Jewish ones, had reopened. German soldiers were trooping in to buy handkerchiefs and sweets, insisting on paying the full price. Even in the Jewish stores. Everywhere they displayed unfailing courtesy. Until that Saturday morning . . .

At precisely ten o'clock, the military commander exited the town hall, flanked by a group of officers in full-dress uniform. The picture of vitality, he bounded onto a rostrum erected for the occasion. He addressed his audience in a gravelly voice:

'The Führer's triumphant army is here to maintain order. It will attend to the security and requirements of the civilian population as long as that population does not jeopardize its own security. At the slightest manifestation of hostility, the German army will deal harshly with the offenders.'

A pale sun suffused the square with gray light. Migratory birds swooped past like ghosts on the run.

'Unfortunately, a serious incident has just occurred,' continued the commander, letting his sharp gaze wander over the assemblage. 'A soldier has been assaulted in the street by a criminal passerby. Fortunately, he was only wounded, and thus able to see his assailant.'

He fell silent, took a breath, and continued:

'The assailant was a Jew.'

From the Poles came a sigh of relief. As for the Jews, they tried to achieve the impossible: to render themselves invisible. Raphael yearned to feel his father's hand on his shoulder, but his father, like all the others, seemed paralyzed.

'Polish citizens,' boomed the commander, 'I have summoned you here this morning, together with the Jews, so that you may recognize the harm they are inflicting upon you. Because of them, you may have to endure hardships you do not deserve. I want you to remember that.'

Among the Poles there were a few notorious anti-Semites who were quick to give the predictable response. It took only an instant for the first one to shout:

'Death to the Jews, death to the Jews! We tolerate them on our soil and those ingrates bring lightning upon our heads! I say, let them croak! The whole lot of them!'

Allowing the agitation to spread, the German commander turned to speak to his subordinates. Then he went on:

'Today we shall set an example. We shall punish the Jewish criminal who dared to attack a soldier wearing the Führer's uniform.'

Responding to a quick motion of his right hand, two soldiers went inside the town hall. They emerged, pushing in front of them a Jew whose face was covered with blood.

'This is a crime that warrants death. And that is what he'll get,' said the commander, looking pleased with himself.

When Raphael saw the condemned man he shuddered. That face, that gait, those eyes, above all, those eyes . . . Could it be? The old man, his friend, the assailant of a German soldier? He remembered the time he lay sick with typhus. He remembered the old man's generosity . . . Meanwhile, soldiers were rushing to erect the gallows. How long did it take them? Ten minutes? A lifetime? Time, for Raphael, had stopped. The sun had stopped shining. Life had lost its meaning.

Hands tied behind his back, the condemned Jew ascended the gallows and faced the assemblage. Was he afraid? If so, he did not show it.

'Are you sure you have nothing to say?' The commander was incredulous.

'Nothing.'

Rabbi Pinhas-the-Great took a step forward:

'Mr Commander, sir, I am a rabbi, one of the rabbis of this community. Since the condemned man is Jewish, surely he is entitled to die as a Jew. I request your permission to let him recite the *Vidui,* the last confession, and the *Shma Israel,* the ancient credo of our martyrs.'

For a moment the officer stared at him as if he were a ghost or a madman. One more word and the rabbi would be shot. But who knows why? Out of respect for the cloth, the rabbi's age, a whim, the commander responded with a single word: 'Fast!'

The rabbi showed surprising agility as he climbed onto the scaffold. As he stood up there, his back partially obscured the assembly's view of the condemned man. But one could see the heads of the two men practically touching. What were they saying? No one could hear. Meanwhile, incredible as it may seem, a whispered debate had been sparked among the Jews: Was it permissible to recite or even to *ask* a Jew to recite the *Vidui* on Shabbat? Someone called on Raphael's father for his opinion, but the teacher was too stunned to respond. Meanwhile, the commander was getting impatient:

'All right, that's enough!'

The rabbi stepped down from the rostrum and took his

place amid the congregation. All eyes were riveted on the condemned man, who was refusing to be blindfolded. The commander was about to issue the fateful order, when the old man's voice rang out:

'Here is my prayer. God of Israel: *Listen to the people of Israel!*'

And so, he had not recited the traditional *Shma* after all, he had not said, *'Listen, Israel, God is one God.'* He had said something else, not the opposite but something else.

Raphael felt guilty. He should have left his parents, if only for a few moments. He should have worked his way forward in the crowd and caught his friend's eye. He should have done something, risked anything, to make the old man understand that he, Raphael, remained his friend, that he would never forget him, never leave him. But he had been a weakling, a coward. And now it was too late . . .

'Wait a minute, my boy. You're not going to get sick again, are you?'

Raphael opened his eyes in astonishment: Thank God. His friend had not been executed by the Germans after all. For there he was, right next to him, smiling. He looked sad, but he was smiling. He had not abandoned him. And no, he had not handed his people over to the enemy.

The old man was speaking. 'Listen, no matter what, you must not get sick again!'

'Yes, but . . .'

'But what?'

'If you are here, who was that on the scaffold?'

The old man did not answer.

Raphael whispered, 'I had to be sure it wasn't you.'

'You're not sure? That's good. I like it that way. Then again, even if it had been me, I would still stay close to you and your family. You see, whenever one of our people dies, I die for him and with him. Oh, I know: it's difficult to understand. Never mind. It's not necessary to understand everything in life, especially at your age.'

Raphael was ten years old.

Perched high on a hill bordered by pine groves and orchards, the Mountain Clinic is like an ancient fortress. Impregnable, mysterious, it dominates the valley and the stream that winds through it.

Far below is the village, one like so many others, with its post office and drugstore, church and library lining its main street. A summer day like so many others. The favorite topic of conversation: the weather. One waits for sun, for rain, for a breeze. One spends one's life waiting. One waits for the children to leave for summer camp, and then one waits for them to return. One waits for the mailman, who brings nothing but bills; for the woman next door, who talks too much, to stop talking, and for her husband, who never opens his mouth, to speak. One waits for a friend who will never come back.

Like me, thinks Raphael. Here I am waiting for someone who may or may not lead me to Pedro, my mentor, my friend. Surely Pedro would help me put my life back together; he would lead me back to the child I once was. For reasons that elude me, I feel guilty toward that boy of ten protected by an old madman who had been dying so long he claimed to be immortal. What is worse than an old madman? A mad child, of course. What do I have in common with that child? Raphael wonders. Am I still drawn to madmen? Is that why I am here at the Mountain Clinic? A thought: And what if my eyes too have become veiled?

Sprawled on his bed, Raphael rubs his temples to try to contain his migraine. It is midafternoon and he should be resting. Like everyone else. But sleep wouldn't help. One cannot run away from one's ghosts. They pursue one right into one's dreams. Better to face them, allow them in. And to follow them to the end. To the crossroads of death and madness. Confusion is the first step. Surely that was the anonymous caller's intent when he slandered Pedro. Doubt is one of Satan's favorite weapons.

Raphael gets up and takes a few uncertain steps, first to the window, then to the door, and finally back to bed. Strange: the door and window have changed places and the room has moved. It is no longer in upstate New York, but on the other side of the ocean, somewhere in Poland. It has become a dark, filthy basement where he is suffocating from the heat, a narrow white cell where he is shivering from the cold.

He watches his brother Hayim being tortured by the Germans, he listens to himself urging the old madman to hurry up and save his brother who is about to die, who is already dead. He finds his brother Yoel rotting in one of Stalin's prisons. 'For God's sake, you have to help him!' he shouts to the old madman, but now *he* is the old madman, and he is helpless like a frail boy of ten who takes on the whole world to prove his best friend innocent.

But the fact is, he no longer wishes to go on living. The small boy of ten refuses to live in a world where the suffering of a friend means so little. He refuses to grow up under the sky of copper and blood that separates God from His creation. Why hasn't the old madman come to his aid? Why hasn't he spoken up? Why isn't he urging him, even now, not to become resigned, not to capitulate to the forces of darkness? Why, why? Raphael hears that word over and over in his mind. Why can't he find some peace? And how long will he have to stay in this wretched place to unmask his enemy?

The Mountain Clinic caters to patients, men and women –

mostly men – whose schizophrenia is linked, in some mysterious way, to Ancient History, to Biblical times. Dr Benedictus, the director, often complains about the lack of space: the establishment can accommodate some fifty patients but has easily ten times that many applicants. 'People don't realize,' he tells anyone willing to listen, 'that this illness has so many variations and is so widespread.'

Being neither a psychiatrist nor a physician, Raphael sometimes feels like a voyeur. All these patients in various states of distress, howling or silent, trying to express their own truths. What right does he have to observe them in their infirmity? But he has no choice: unless he takes a stand against the enemy, justice will not be done. If he does not defend Pedro's honor, life will become meaningless. He must find redemption among these prophets and judges, princes and martyrs. There are also several messiahs here, indulging their vanity, their bitterness. Two reigning kings receive their subjects. One is threatened by his stillborn heir, the other by his senile stepfather. Aristophanes weeps, Socrates laughs. Caligula takes himself for his horse. To live in this clinic amid all these hallucinated characters is to relive the turbulence and upheaval of Ancient Civilization. Here, madness and history flow into each other, each feeding the other's delirium.

'In the beginning there was madness,' says Dr Benedictus ponderously.

'Not the Word?' wonders Raphael.

'No. Madness . . .'

Thereupon he launches into an elaborate monologue on the genesis of dementia and its influence on history. Schizoid behavior and paranoid reactions, transference and repression, the Oedipus complex, the Icarus complex, Freudian versus Jungian analysis. It seems that he has not only read all the books on the subject but has also rewritten them. 'Of course,' he continues, 'Christianity believes that in the beginning was the Word. But before the Word, what was there? Chaos? But what is chaos if not the loss of perception, sensitivity, language? A total pathological retrenchment. Before Creation, there was a vision of the future, and I tell you, that vision could originate only in great madness.'

'You sound like a mystic, not a psychiatrist,' says Raphael.

The director looks annoyed. He shrugs.

'That may be. But only because mysticism is one of our concerns. We recognize that mysticism is, in a manner of speaking, relevant to psychiatry.'

'And what, in a manner of speaking, is psychiatry relevant to?' asks Raphael petulantly.

'Everything,' states Benedictus categorically. 'We try to return the patient to his true center. Push any man to the limit of his strength or his patience, or his faith, and there ensues a critical mental imbalance that necessitates psychiatric intervention. What intrigues me is that while the mystic may need the psychiatrist, the psychiatrist does not seem to need the mystic.'

'And God?' asks Raphael quietly.

'What about God?' snaps the director.

'Does God need either one, the mystic or the psychiatrist?'

'We could put the question directly to him,' responds Benedictus. 'The Almighty has done us the honor of seeking our help. He lives right under this roof, you know.'

And he bursts into laughter.

'Listen, God. What I am about to tell you is for your own good. Stop! Yes, God: Stop this senseless project. Believe me, even you who are omnipotent cannot succeed in this. You thought man would be your glory, the jewel of your crown.

You make me laugh. Man is your failure. Face it. Give up your illusions. Wake up. Be considerate: Close the book before you turn the first page. Does it shame you to admit that I'm right? Then forget it's my idea. Let it be my gift to you. Legally, philosophically, you will have fathered it. And you know what? Theologically too. All you have to say is: I tried, I was wrong. And, luckily for the world, I realized it in time. Thus, even if your dream will have lasted but one day, one lifetime, you will be applauded. By your angels and seraphim. By the countless souls who will escape the curse of being born only to die. By the trees that will not be felled by man. By the animals that will not be slaughtered. By the earth that will not be despoiled. And all of Creation, pure and resplendent, will say: Look how great is God, how admirable His honesty. He does not shrink from admitting His error. And yes, He can manage perfectly well without man . . .

'So, tell me, God: do you accept my proposition? Will you take back your design for man? It's not too late. Nobody will know, I guarantee it. I'll be discreet, I promise, cross my heart and hope to die. I shall never betray your secret, our secret. Nobody will bear you a grudge for nobody will ever find out. One day you will thank me, you'll see. One must learn to admit failure, even when one is God . . .'

On his knees, hands clasped in a gesture of supplication, Adam looks like a clown begging for laughter. And yet everybody knows he is a great scholar, a genius perhaps. Therefore difficult to live with, so difficult that he severed his ties to his parents while still in high school. And in college he managed to antagonize all his professors. His wedding night was spent alone, his bride having slammed the door on him and his cosmic discoveries.

He was the first patient Raphael had met at the clinic. 'He thinks he is Adam,' the director had said. 'God remains his favorite interlocutor, his only interlocutor. Other mortals barely exist for him. The only patient he acknowledges is "God."'

The man has the haunted look of a fugitive.

'Adam,' says Raphael, 'are you afraid of me?'

While waiting for Adam to answer, Raphael looks around the room. He is struck by its sparseness. Not a single photograph or treasured object. Emptiness, he tolerates only emptiness. Dr Benedictus has told Raphael that the mere sight of man-made things – paintings, furniture – offends him, puts him into a rage.

'Can't you see I'm busy? Leave me alone,' he growls.

Through the window, the garden seems distant, unnaturally bright. A man sits on a bench, counting his fingers. Across from him, a woman endlessly combs her hair. Two nurses are engrossed in conversation, oblivious of their surroundings.

'Adam, are you afraid of me?' Raphael asks again.

Adam laughs. 'It's you who is afraid of *me*. Admit it. Have the courage to admit it.'

Raphael chooses his words carefully. 'If it pleases you . . .'

'Don't pretend you're here to please me. You're here to frighten me. I know it and you know it. Only you haven't planned this well. You see? One can be God and still plan things poorly. You want to know why? Because man is involved. And that changes everything. As soon as man appears, the game becomes rigged. That is why I appeal to your wisdom: give up this project! You don't need man. Not even me. Reverse yourself. Turn me back into a grain of sand. A speck of dust.'

With his sharp profile, dark curly hair, he looks younger than forty. Raphael knows something about his life, but not the essential facts. Anyway, what is essential in a madman?

In the Far East, long ago, Raphael came upon a wild-eyed beggar who asked him for alms. Ashamed, Raphael whispered,

'Sorry, I'm just as poor as you are.' The man smiled. 'Thank you. Thank you, friend, for your gift.' Raphael didn't understand. 'But I haven't given you anything.' The man shook his head. 'Oh, yes, you have, my friend. You gave me your honesty. And also your poverty. You gave me your trust.'

'You are God and I am your creature,' says Adam, interrupting Raphael's thoughts. 'Yet we fear one another. And that fear is our link. Was that your motive? Could it be that you created man merely to frighten him?'

Raphael has no answer.

'Is it wrong, Pedro, is it wrong to think constantly of God? And to see him in others?'

'What is wrong is to think of God while forgetting man.'

'I have not forgotten man.'

'Yes, you have. To live means to forget. In order to taste freedom, I must forget prison. To be more precise: I am incapable of savoring my freedom unless I forget prison. To recall one companion is to forget the others. Again and again, a writer chooses one word at the expense of all others. As for you, you listen to Adam so as not to listen to your parents, your brothers, your daughter. You evoke God so as to turn your back on man.'

'That's not true,' I protest. 'You're unfair. You're trying to hurt me. Why, Pedro?'

'You don't understand. I'm trying to bring you back to life. If in so doing I hurt you, I'm sorry.'

'Are you angry with me for forgetting the dead?'

'No. Just don't forget the living.'

Suddenly Pedro's face is close to mine. For one long moment he stares at me silently. I meet his gaze but quickly lower my eyes as he continues in his deep, resonant voice: 'What do you expect to find in this clinic? What truth do you hope to take away from here? And what will you do with it?'

I don't answer. I don't know how to answer. The real reason for my coming here still eludes me. Or does it? Maybe I'm just ashamed.

Has Pedro guessed as much? If so, he doesn't let on. He continues:

'Remember. Remember that the misunderstood writer is often considered mad. The storyteller no one listens to is thought to have said nothing. The believer scorned by God is but a dangerous dreamer. And then, this too: A man without fear is a man without love.'

Has Pedro too gone mad?

Stepping off the bus, Raphael looks around for a taxi. If only he hadn't missed the train at Grand Central, the director's driver would have been here to pick him up. He probably should have informed the clinic that he would come by bus. He can't remember why he didn't. Either he was out of change or all the pay phones were broken. Never mind, here he is, at the village bus stop. He goes into the coffee shop, orders a black coffee, and asks the waitress behind the counter where the taxi stand is.

'There isn't any,' says the waitress.

'No stand or no taxis?'

'There's one taxi, just one.'

Raphael shrugs as if to say, Oh, well, I guess we're pretty far from Manhattan.

'Forget the taxi,' says the waitress. 'The owner's an old drunk. He's probably sleeping it off somewhere. I'll call the clinic. They'll send someone down for you.'

Raphael watches her dial the number, hears her mumble something. He wonders: How did she know where he was going? What is she telling them? And why is she glancing at him like that? He gulps down his coffee. She hangs up.

'The car will be here in ten minutes.'

Raphael thanks her, steps outside. It is midafternoon. Children are on their way home from school. Two young women sit on a stoop talking. Down the street an old man naps on a bench. A soothing silence hangs over the village. What peace, thinks Raphael, my God, what peace. One dare not disturb it with a jarring reference, an inappropriate thought. Yet he feels a gnawing uneasiness. What if the caller deliberately put him on a false trail? And what if they decided to keep him at the clinic indefinitely, a patient among patients, a living ruin among ancient ruins? If only Pedro were here to help him understand.

A car pulls up, putting an end to his meditation. The young nurse at the wheel is pretty. Huge black eyes, auburn hair pulled back into a bun. 'My name is Karen,' she says. 'Please get in.' They drive several miles without passing another car and without exchanging a word.

'Is it much farther?' asks Raphael, just to say something.

'Not really.'

'At least you don't have a traffic problem.'

No answer. Not even a smile to reward his pitiful attempt.

'Have you been working at the clinic long?'

'Yes.'

'It can't be *that* long.'

'Thanks for the compliment.'

Not talkative, this nurse. Too bad, thinks Raphael. He likes nurses.

She stops the car at the top of a hill, gets out. Raphael follows her. 'The director asked me to show you around. So don't get any ideas.'

Raphael blushes. He is in no mood to flirt. Or to admire the scenery, for that matter. Still, the view is magnificent. A valley in bloom. Dense, mysterious forests. A blue sky suggesting infinite solitude, the genesis of dreams, the death of winter, the death of death.

They return to the car and continue their journey. A few minutes later they stop before an iron gate. Karen honks the horn. The gate opens. The car makes its way up a long, winding drive. At the top of the hill is a sprawling ivy-covered building with massive black doors.

'What about my things?'

'They'll be brought to your room.'

The heavy doors open. A cheerful, ruddy-faced nurse shows Raphael to the director's office. Standing behind a perfectly ordered desk, a tall, gray-haired man in an impeccable suit holds out his hand.

'I'm Dr Benedictus. Welcome to the Mountain Clinic. We were expecting you this morning.'

'I'm sorry, I missed my train.'

The director motions him toward the sofa, offers him a cold drink, and immediately begins to question him: 'Since you are going to work here, we must get to know each other.'

Raphael is amused. The director thinks he's being clever. Surely he has pored over his papers and already knows all he needs to know. As he is being examined, Raphael sizes up his examiner.

The director asks what Raphael considers a loaded question:

'Tell me, Professor, what made you choose our clinic over all the others?'

Raphael has his answer ready:

'Its reputation, of course. Everyone knows the Mountain Clinic is the best of its kind.'

The director nods approvingly and the conversation turns to how Raphael will spend his time. Raphael tells the director he intends to explore the relationship between madness and prophecy, between the madmen of the Bible and today's mad-men, their diverse responses to their common despair. He hopes to uncover hidden meanings, arrive at a synthesis, and develop it into an essay for one of the scholarly journals. In other words, he has come to observe, to listen, to learn.

What a good liar I am, he thinks. *I've learned to lie well, haven't I, Pedro?*

'Let us summarize,' says the director. 'You'll stay with us for approximately three months. Until September, you'll be part of our team. You'll be lodged and fed. You'll also be entitled to a modest stipend.'

Raphael begins to protest.

'I know, I know,' says Benedictus. 'You don't expect to be paid. But in my establishment there are only two categories: staff, who are paid, and patients, who pay. Since you don't seem ill, you'll be paid.'

'Then how can I be of help to you?'

'Our librarian has been on leave for several months. Perhaps you could restore some order to our library. Apart from that, I'm sure your knowledge of the Bible will be invaluable to us. Of course, that was one of the reasons we were so interested in having you here.'

Once more, Raphael tries to read the expression on the director's face. Is he making fun of him? Is he setting a trap? No, he seems sincere. But what about his voice? No, he does not have an accent like the caller.

'I'm confident that our arrangement will work out to our mutual satisfaction,' says the director, rising from his chair. 'You will be able to pursue your research; and we will be able to use our library again. You'll find the atmosphere here more conducive to work than the university. I know something about that . . . Ah, here is Karen. She'll show you to your room.'

*

The Feast of Lights, 1940. Under a blanket of snow, the ghetto barely breathed. The Biblical curses had become reality. Nights were spent waiting for dawn; days were spent waiting for dusk. Hunger was etched into the faces. Behind darkened windows lurked terror. Still, one got used to everything. Including death, which by now was often met with resignation, even indifference. One only escorted the deceased a few paces before turning back. One no longer wept. There was no strength left for mourning the dead. The need to mourn the living was too great.

Aharon and his family occupied a room in a dilapidated structure that had once belonged to a relative. That was the rule: one family per room. During the day, the Lipkins' room also served as *heder*. Every morning a dozen schoolboys arrived to study the sacred tongue, the laws and tales of the Bible. If one listened closely, their tentative voices could be heard in the street. Now and then a passerby would stop, wipe away an errant tear, and continue on his way. Aharon interrupted his class only when the lookout spotted a German.

When Rabbi Pinhas commended him on his devotion, he replied: 'I owe it to the children, I owe it to our people. What would the Jewish people be without its children?'

'But still, Aharon, the danger . . .'

Respectfully, he reminded Rabbi Pinhas of the Talmudic stories about sages who, during the Roman occupation, stopped children in the streets to ask what they had learned in school that day. 'What would have happened if the children had said they had learned nothing?'

'Aharon, Aharon,' replied Rabbi Pinhas, smiling sadly, 'do you really expect our sages of long ago to come walking through our ghetto?'

'If they do, Rabbi Pinhas, my pupils will be prepared.'

And prepared they were. Though they were often hungry

and sick, the Jewish children tirelessly repeated after their master the verses that had been handed down from generation to generation for three thousand years.

'Remember, children,' Aharon told them, 'our ancestors were starved, persecuted, tortured in Egypt. But God, blessed-be-He, needed them. He needed their faith, their testimony, and above all, their memory. For that reason, they survived their enemies. Now we too shall survive.'

Of course the ranks were getting thinner. Children died from hunger and exhaustion. Entire families disappeared. But throughout it all the *heder* remained open.

On the last night of Hanukkah, the schoolboys joined the Lipkins in lighting the eighth and final candle. They sang the traditional songs, and, later, Rivka and her daughters served roasted potatoes. The schoolboys were happy. Oh, yes, one could be happy in the ghetto.

When the pupils left, Rivka collapsed onto the bed. 'What will happen to us?' she cried. 'How long must we go on like this?'

'Patience, Rivka,' said Aharon. 'Be patient. We are alive, that in itself is a miracle. Let us be grateful to the Lord for that.'

A heavy silence hung over the room. The candles flickered slowly. Shadows lengthened on the walls. Ruth was thinking of her Mendel, whose last letter from Tomaszov had spoken of illness. Her sister Esther was mending socks. As for Raphael, his eyes were fixed on Hayim. He knew his brother was about to say something serious, he even knew what he was going to say, for Hayim had confided in him the night before.

Hayim walked over to the candles, played with them absently. Raphael encouraged him with his eyes: Go ahead, Hayim, tell them, tell us what's on your mind. It's now or never. In response to his younger brother's insistent gaze, Hayim turned to face his family.

He addressed himself to Aharon. 'I've come to a decision, Father.'

All eyes were on him. He seemed more tense than ever and thinner too. Rivka stared at her son, a worried look on her face. Was he ill? What was he planning? Who could know with such a dreamer?

'I am leaving,' said Hayim quietly.

All but Raphael gasped. Leaving? Where did he think he could go? Surely he knew that the ghetto, fenced with barbed wire, was a place one left only with the Germans' permission.

'I'm going to Palestine,' said Hayim.

Aharon sank into a chair. Esther froze, her needle midair. Ruth looked nervously from her father to her mother, as if to read on their faces the meaning of what she had just heard. Rivka was shaking her head as if to say, No, not possible, she would not permit such madness.

'Father,' said Hayim, 'please listen and try to understand. It's not that I want to run away. That's not the point.'

Aharon looked at his son. The sadness in his eyes had deepened. 'What *is* the point, Hayim?'

'Palestine. The Holy Land. You know that I've been dreaming of going there for years. As a Zionist, I believe that one of our family must be there, if only to pave the way.'

The last candle went out. Ruth got up with a sigh and lit the oil lamp. Lost in thought, Aharon rubbed his chin.

'Palestine is far away,' he said at last. 'How in God's name do you hope to get there?'

Hayim, relieved that the conversation was taking a practical turn, launched into a lengthy explanation. His movement was planning a breakout from the ghetto. Ten of his friends, boys and girls, were involved. Passersby were standing ready to help them cross the Hungarian border. On the other side, comrades would be waiting to drive them to Romania. In Constanza they would board a ship. A few days later they would be in Haifa. Nothing to it.

Hayim expected questions, but nobody was asking any.

'Hayim,' said Aharon, after a long silence.

'Yes, Father?'

'Your brother and sisters, take them with you.'

Rivka jumped. 'What? Nobody is going anywhere. Besides, that's no trip for girls!'

Aharon tried to reason with her.

'I also love them, you know that, they know that. And yet, they may have to live far away. Who knows what the future holds? The situation is getting worse every day. The war will not be over so soon. If the children have an opportunity to escape, let them go.'

Rivka looked at him with tender disbelief. She started to speak but changed her mind. Had her husband persuaded her? Or had she given up?

'I want to stay here,' said Raphael, going over to his mother, taking her hand.

'So do we,' said the sisters.

Hayim felt the tears well up. Even if his sisters wanted to leave, he could not take them. The instructions were clear: only members could go on this journey. But then, why the tears? Why did he feel so guilty? For leaving his family behind? Thank God the room was almost dark. No one would see him cry.

'Hayim,' said Aharon. 'When you're in Jerusalem, you won't forget to pray for us, will you?'

'He won't forget,' said Raphael.

In the days that followed, Raphael did not leave his brother's side.

'Try to grow up fast,' Hayim told Raphael. 'Our parents are not so young anymore. Take good care of them, and of the girls. I know you're only eleven, but these days everything is upside down. Children manage better than adults. With Yoel in Lvov and Ezra in Lodz, you'll be in charge. I know I can count on you.'

Together they walked through the winding streets of the ghetto. Swathed in old bedsheets or tattered overcoats, the passersby all looked like beggars, while real beggars whispered, their palms outstretched, 'Have mercy, mercy.'

'In one month,' said Raphael, 'where will you be? Will you already be in Palestine?'

'I hope so,' said Hayim.

'What do you think it will be like?'

'It will be beautiful. Sunny skies. Blue sea. Green mountains. Jews who are free to laugh, sing, dream.'

'Go on,' said Raphael. 'Tell me more.'

'Boys and girls on a kibbutz, working the land, learning to be farmers, shepherds, craftsmen. Come sunset, they gather under a tree to recite the *Minhah* prayer. And up above, the angels are smiling.'

'Go on, please tell me more,' said Raphael.

'Jerusalem . . . I imagine Jerusalem in all its splendor, in all its majesty. To me it is the soul of the Jewish people. I imagine it and my heart begins to pound. As I approach the Wall, I hear steps behind me. I turn around and all of you are there, following me. I reach the Wall, I kiss its weathered stones. I look around, I look for you, I look for all of you. But I am alone . . .'

Hayim stopped short, frightened by his own vision. 'You will follow me, won't you, Raphael? Do you promise?'

'I promise.'

'And you'll bring Mother and Father? And Ruth and Esther? And maybe even Yoel and Ezra?'

'I promise.'

But when Hayim left the ghetto one week later, he was sure he would never see his family again.

A Jewish policeman helped him cross to the other side, where he was met by a comrade who escorted him to the next village. By morning, the whole group would be assembled. The guide who would take them to the Hungarian border, one hundred twenty kilometers away, was due at midnight. The plan was to move by night and hide in the woods by day.

For once, God was on their side: a blizzard kept the guards from making their rounds, and the group crossed the border undetected. A comrade was waiting for them on Hungarian soil. A few hours later, in Szerencsefalu, Hayim was an honored guest at the home of Reb Yankel, a prosperous merchant, a pillar of his community.

At that time, Hungarian Jews were still leading a relatively carefree life. Though pro-German, the government had not yet adopted Nazi policy. Jews continued to live in their houses, to carry on with their business, to circulate freely between cities, even to travel abroad. Hungary became a haven for Polish refugees. And so, the Jews who lived near the border were kept busy.

The system worked smoothly. Refugees were sheltered long enough to be provided with false papers. Then they were smuggled to Budapest or even as far as Romania. While waiting for their documents, Hayim and his friends were encouraged to participate in community affairs. They attended synagogue and tried to be of service wherever they could. Hayim offered to bind Reb Yankel's books, and the merchant gratefully accepted. Then, miracle of miracles, one day while he was working, Reb Yankel's daughter Rika walked into the library. She was shy, graceful, and he promptly fell in love with her. Nothing like this had ever happened to him before. He felt guilty. He felt like a thief. He avoided his host. He stopped eating; he stopped sleeping. Lying awake in the early-morning hours, he tried desperately to concentrate on his parents, on Raphael, so as to take his mind off the young girl. He was miserable; he had never been so miserable.

One morning when Rika brought him breakfast, he immediately saw her as his wife. Together they would build a home. In Palestine, of course. And what if she refused to leave her family? Never mind, they would go to Palestine later. His dreams collapsed the next day when he was informed that all was ready for the journey. That very day. A refugee must learn to obey. A refugee must learn to forget. To detach himself from people, places, habits. Did Rika know that he loved her? If so, she did not show it. Which was just as well because Hayim would not have known how to behave if she had.

All right . . . Time to take leave of Reb Yankel. There were still books to be bound? Sorry, but . . . Reb Yankel clasped his hand. May God keep you, son. He offered him some money. At first Hayim refused. But when Reb Yankel insisted, he let himself be persuaded. The whole household was gathered by the open gate. Everyone looked sad, the young girl most of all.

Good-bye, good-bye. May God keep you. Will you remember us in Palestine? Of course I'll remember you in Palestine. A comrade called to him that it was getting late. The train . . . They had to take the train to Nagyvarad, the border. His comrade was tugging at his sleeve. They had to hurry.

Hayim closed the gate and headed for the station. It was a beautiful spring day. The other members of the group were waiting on the platform. 'We thought you'd never make it.'

A sharp whistle. The train arrives in a cloud of steam. The group splits up, three to a compartment. I will never again see this station, this town, thinks Hayim. I will never again see Reb Yankel, his house, his library. Never mind Reb Yankel, I will never again see his daughter, his lovely daughter. Abruptly his thoughts go to his parents. I will never again see my family. He wants to turn back. He wants to take Rika to meet his parents. All aboard! The train lurches forward. With his life.

But Hayim was mistaken. What had happened? A whim or a sudden stiffening of official policy? One hour after it had left Szerencsefalu, policemen boarded the train and conducted a search. Hayim and his friends carried false papers and spoke not a word of Hungarian. At the next station they were taken off the train. And the following day they were back in Szerencsefalu, handcuffed and under heavy guard.

The news spread quickly through the Jewish community. Friends and allies were alerted. Official connections were brought into play. In vain. Hayim and his comrades were charged with espionage and treason. The Jews were warned not to interfere. This matter was considered grave, so grave that Budapest itself was kept informed. This did not deter the Jewish community from moving heaven and earth to help their young friends.

The investigation was conducted by Captain Fehér, an accomplished brute, an expert in the art of torture. His questions hit the prisoners like machine-gun fire: 'Who organized the illegal border crossing? Who forged the papers? Where did the money come from? Who was the mastermind? And who were his accomplices?' He repeated his questions ten times, a hundred times, while striking his victims on the head or kicking them in the groin. The nails he left to the end. He tore them out slowly, one by one, to allow the prisoners time to imagine what lay ahead.

At first the prisoners suffered and didn't speak; then they suffered and did speak. If anyone ever tells you that it is possible to resist torture, that it is possible to remain silent indefinitely, do not believe him. The torturer is always stronger than the victim. The victim's only recourse is to faint. But that's not so easy. Not easy to lose consciousness at the first blow, to slip into oblivion while the torturer is whipping your face, to remain numb while cigarette butts are ground into your chest. Only sometimes the torturer does not stop in time. Bent on extracting a full confession, he pushes the victim until he collapses.

By a miracle of bravery, the prisoners did not reveal the names of the Hungarian Jews who had helped them. Instead, they gave elaborate descriptions of their activities in Poland. Captain Fehér threatened them: 'You think you're deceiving me, you're not. I'll soon have the answers. Or else, you'll die.'

The community dispatched a delegate to Budapest to intercede with the War Ministry. And another to plead with the Ministry of the Interior. A substantial sum was collected to bribe any high official ready to cooperate.

In the meantime, the Jewish leaders of Szerencsefalu had obtained the right to visit the prisoners. They were allowed to bring them kosher food, at first once, then twice a day; and were thus able to pass on news and messages. For a fee, policemen relaxed the rules. The visits stretched from five minutes to fifteen. And then something unexpected happened to Hayim: one day Rika appeared bearing food and messages. She looked into his eyes, wanting to know everything. Not only for herself but for her father and the others. They needed to know what methods of torture Captain Fehér was using. A complaint had been filed in Budapest, and the officials were demanding particulars. Hayim was embarrassed. How could he tell this innocent young girl that the captain took particular pleasure in kicking his private parts? And so he guiltily left out this 'detail'. Anyway, he preferred looking at her to speaking. But she didn't see it that way. He must talk. She insisted on it. And so he talked: the first torture session, the second, the fainting spells, the brutal awakenings. The more he spoke, the more she loved him. At least, that is what he imagined. How could she fail to love him since he loved her so?

She did love him, but in her own way. She loved him because she pitied him. She had never met anyone who had endured such torture. She had never known anyone for whom there was so little hope. For she knew what Hayim did not, that in spite of all the efforts in high places, the chances of obtaining their release were slim. As a last resort, the community was trying to have them transferred to the capital. Anything was better than deportation back to Poland. Yet that was precisely what was in store for them.

While Hayim was in prison, the government had decreed the deportation to Poland of all Jewish 'aliens' in Hungary. Twelve hundred people fell into that category in Szerencsefalu alone. At the last moment, the chief of police had ordered Hayim's name and those of his comrades added to the list.

Once again, Hayim was headed for the station, this time never to return. But contrary to what he had thought when he left the ghetto, he was to see his family again.

Raphael has no idea why Cain stares at him that way. What is clear is that he is in a rage, a murderous rage. Not that Raphael is afraid. If he becomes violent, Raphael will restrain him. If necessary, he will call one of the male nurses. Cain seems unable to keep still: he gets up, sits down, stands up again, rushes to the window, curses the garden and those who walk in it, the earth and all its inhabitants. The only son of a Cleveland industrialist, he has become fixated on the idea that he once had a brother whom he murdered.

'Did you do that?' asks Raphael, looking at him gravely. 'Did you really murder your brother?'

'What else could I do?' Cain replies. 'I had no choice.'

'One can always choose not to kill.'

'That's what you think. Just listen. One day my father decides that I should give him my most cherished possession: my gold watch. I agree, of course. After all, he is my father. He is entitled to whatever is mine. Only no sooner do I bring him my watch than he refuses it. Why? Because he has changed his mind. He now has a new whim. He no longer wants a watch. Not even my beautiful gold watch. What he wants now is a red leather notebook. The very one I gave my brother for his birthday. And my dear brother, that little bastard, what does he do? Without a word to me, he rushes to his room, grabs his precious notebook, and brings it to my father. Who accepts it, of course, and carries on about how grateful, how proud, he is to have such a generous son. Tell me, is that fair? Is that right? Suddenly my beautiful gold watch has become worthless. The mere sight of it makes me sick. And who's to blame? I ask you. Do you still wonder that I'm angry? That I yearn to destroy everything, to burn the holy altars and kill the priests? You look shocked. Don't be. Cain is Cain because he believes in justice!'

He had been popular at school, but never with his father. Among other things, his father disapproved of his concern for others:

'You think people will thank you? They'll laugh at you and your pathological kindness.' Yes, that was the term the Cleveland industrialist had used: pathological kindness.

His son was aghast:

'Are you saying that kindness is a disease? That compassion for the poor is a weakness? I don't understand you, Father.'

But just as he did not understand his father, his father did not understand him. His mother refused to get involved. As long as her son loved her, nothing else mattered. So what if he rushed to the defense of a bullied classmate? Or helped a friend with his homework? Or shared his allowance? As long as he loved her, nothing else mattered.

Then one day his father found one hundred dollars missing from his wallet.

'I'm calling the police,' thundered the industrialist. 'I will not have a thief under my roof!'

'But the money was not for me; I have everything I need. I took it for a friend who was hungry.'

'Nonsense. Nobody goes hungry in America.'

'You're wrong, Father.'

'Oh, no, I'm not. The only ones who go hungry are the derelicts who choose to buy drugs and whiskey instead of bread. It's time you woke up to such things. Your friend not only deceived you, he drove you to steal from me. Next you'll steal from a stranger. And when you end up in prison, just don't count on me to bail you out.'

That evening, he overheard his mother say, 'Maybe this is our fault. Maybe if he'd had a brother or a sister . . .'

He felt like storming into their bedroom and shouting, 'You fools! That has nothing to do with anything. Whether or not I am an only child is of no importance to anyone – including me. I don't want a brother or a sister. All I want is to be left alone.'

Raphael listens attentively, trying to fathom what could have provoked Cain's anguished fantasies. It was a total mystery. 'How old are you?' he asks.

'What's it to you?'

'How old were you when you killed your brother?'

'Old enough to know what I was doing.'

'And your brother, how old was he when he died?'

'He didn't tell me. What do you think of that? Nor did I ask him. Besides, who told you that he's dead? I tell you: I killed him, but he is still alive. That way I can kill him over and over again.'

Suddenly, his face is close to Raphael's. 'And anyway, what business is it of yours? I don't even know who you are,' he screams. 'I've never seen you before. Tell me: Who are you?'

When Raphael doesn't answer, he shouts:

'Don't you play games with me. I know who you are. You can't deceive me. They tricked me once, they won't do it again . . . As for you, dear little brother, don't be a fool. I'll strangle you with my bare hands if I have to. And don't count on the nurses to save you. I'm stronger than they are. And don't count on God. The way I feel right now, I'm capable of killing Him too.'

'God?' asks Raphael. 'Why God?'

'Don't ask me. Ask God. When I killed my brother, it was really Him I wanted to kill. And He knows it. Any fool knows that whoever kills, kills God.'

The patient turns his gaze toward the garden. 'I hate man,' he growls. 'He poisons everything he touches.'

'Would you like me to leave you alone now?'

'I am alone. Your presence has no bearing on my solitude.'

Cain looks drained. He is shaking. With his delicate hands, his sensitive eyes, he looks like a poet or an artist, a victim rather than a killer.

No, this was not how Raphael had imagined Cain.

*

Yoel had not received his parents' telegram. In the chaos of war, nothing worked. The cable system was no exception. Yoel solicited his friends' opinion: to return to Rovidok or to stay in Lvov? Before he had time to make up his mind, the Red Army was at the city gates. When Poland surrendered, only a few Jewish refugees accepted Soviet permission to go back to what was now the German-occupied zone. For Yoel, a sympathizer of the clandestine Communist movement who saw in the Soviet regime the possibility of true freedom, the decision would have been easy had it not been for his family in Rovidok. Of course, the Jews of Lvov had no choice: it was occupation or almost certain death. For the Jews of Lvov all exits were blocked.

The last three years in Lvov had been relatively comfortable for Yoel. Though he still practiced his religion, he had felt the pull of emancipation. He had begun to visit secular libraries and cultural centers, to meet other young people, and without actually becoming a Party member, he had undeniably fallen under its influence – to some degree because of a young girl named Mirele, who had embraced communism as her religion.

Mirele's fervor was even more remarkable than her beauty. Once you heard her recite a revolutionary poem in Yiddish, you could never forget her. Her voice was warm and seductive. The boys fell in love just listening to her.

Yoel was seeing her more and more often. He worked for her father, Shlomo Reichmann, who owned the largest bookshop in Lvov. A vocal proponent of Jewish emancipation, Reichmann had offered a job to the young man from Rovidok for reasons that were unclear, even to himself. Did he think he could succeed in weaning him from the more fanatic practices of his faith? Was he secretly impressed by the young man's erudition in Jewish subjects? Did he see in him a prospective son-in-law?

Shlomo Reichmann was a widower who had lost his wife when Mirele was five. His daughter was his whole life. He had fended off opportunities to remarry and had brought her up alone. Their relationship was one of tenderness and complicity. In the presence of strangers, they would often exchange winks and knowing smiles.

Yoel had great respect for Reichmann, a respect that soon turned into admiration. Even though, for someone with Yoel's background, the bookdealer's quest for freedom bordered on heresy.

Shlomo Reichmann considered himself a historian, more precisely *the* historian of the Jewish community of Lvov. Whenever he was not with his customers, he threw himself into the piles of documents and chronicles he had discovered over the years in the various archives of the city. No wonder he was not only nearsighted but hunchbacked too. He carried the weight of centuries on his shoulders.

'To everyone his enemy,' he told Yoel as they worked side by side in his shop. 'Mine is time. It tries to erase everything. I try to hold it back. What a struggle we are engaged in! Still, I manage to snatch a few fateful moments. To avenge itself, time wants to push me into oblivion. But I won't let it happen. We historians are fighters and our weapon is memory. If we learn how to use it, we will win.'

Yoel was astonished. For him, history was the failed sacrifice of Isaac, the solitary death of Moses, the ambiguous relations between Saul and David, the tragedy of King Zedekiah. It, was also the teachings of Hillel and Shammai, the adventures of Rabbi Shimon, son of Yohai – but Lvov? Why would Lvov, albeit Jewish Lvov and its history, interest him?

'Did you know, Yoel, that the first Jews to settle in our city came from Byzantium? And that they were quite prosperous here? One day, one day, I'll lay my hands on one of their wedding contracts and then . . .'

When he was excited, Shlomo Reichmann had a habit of not finishing his sentences. They seemed to amble through his dreams, searching for a chance to blossom. In truth, Yoel was often at a loss to understand the bookdealer's enthusiasm. There were Byzantine Jews in Lvov? Hooray for them and hooray for Lvov! Why on earth would this information concern him? There were Jews everywhere, there would always be Jews everywhere. Was that not the law of Jewish history? The Lord will disperse the Jewish people among other nations for its own good, said the Talmud. They had made their way to Persia and Babylon and Rome; why wouldn't they have reached Lvov?

'Did you know, Yoel, that the Karaites established a colony in Lvov, and that it flourished until 1457? Here, take a look at this document . . . and this one . . .'

The bookdealer's face radiated happiness and pride. He was in his element. And gradually, his passion began to affect Yoel, who was going to learn more about the Karaites than he had ever thought possible: about Anan, their founder, and his disciples; his disagreements with Rav Sadia Gaon, his shortlived triumphs, his memorable arguments. That the Karaites denied the oral tradition seemed sacrilegious to Yoel. For him, the Talmud sprang from the same divinely inspired source as the Bible. Not so for Shlomo Reichmann. A consummate rationalist, he considered the Talmud an interesting document, no more, no less. He accepted some of its laws, but rejected others, admired one legend while dismissing another as a charming fable. He loved to teach Yoel, hoping thus to pull him, step by step, out of his world of darkness and superstition. He wanted Yoel to acknowledge the humanist lessons of

Judaism. The more he resisted, the more Reichmann aspired to save him.

Of course, for Yoel, the bookdealer's greatest asset was not his erudition but his daughter Mirele. Yoel found her attractive in more ways than one. Never before had he heard a young girl speak so freely in the presence of her father. Never before had he seen a young girl as a person and not as a creature apart.

When, at what precise moment, did he realize he was in love with Mirele? Was it the morning he surprised her in the kitchen, her braids undone, her silky hair falling to her shoulders? He found her so beautiful and mysterious that he almost forgot to breathe. Once, he watched her as she sat on the veranda, her head bent over a book. Absorbed in her reading, she did not notice him. Her beauty so troubled him that he tiptoed out of the room for fear of making a fool of himself. Another time, she arrived at the bookshop while her father and Yoel were discussing the role of Shabbat in Jewish tradition. Shlomo interpreted it as a social phenomenon, whereas Yoel viewed it as a gift from God. Yoel spoke quietly. The bookdealer shouted.

'Father,' said Mirele, 'why are you shouting?'

'To make him understand that . . .'

'Father! You think he'll understand you better if you shout?'

'Wait a minute, Mirele. It's your father you should be defending.'

'You don't need to be defended, Father. Whenever you argue, you summon three thousand years of history to defend you.'

There was so much love for her in her father's eyes that Yoel felt strangely uneasy. He had never really thought about love. Thou shalt love God, thou shalt love thy neighbor, thou shalt love the stranger. What exactly did that mean: to love? Until he met Mirele, he thought he knew the answer: to love meant to work on behalf of another, to do good deeds to please God, to study Torah, to make one's parents happy. But it was no longer that simple. How could he express his love for Mirele? More importantly, how could he hide it? Not knowing what to do, he blushed. He blushed every time he was in her presence. He even blushed when they were apart. He had only to recall the way she laughed, the way she walked, and his whole body was on fire.

During those weeks, Yoel immersed himself in his work at the bookshop. Nights were given over to his correspondence – long weekly letters to his parents, with messages for his brothers and sisters. He would not admit it, but he missed his family. In fact, he was so homesick that he was more than once on the verge of leaving Lvov, of going home. But there was Mirele.

One evening she found him alone in the dining room, where he often worked because his own room was too small for a table. The dining room was always being transformed to meet different needs, serving alternately as classroom, meeting hall, study.

'What are you doing?' asked Mirele.

He looked up, startled. 'Oh, nothing.'

'You're writing?'

'To my parents.'

'In what language do you write?'

'In Yiddish.'

'My father hasn't converted you to Hebrew yet?'

'No, not yet.'

Being an enlightened Jew, a Maskil, Shlomo Reichmann often drew wistful smiles for his determination to revive Hebrew as a spoken language at the expense of Yiddish. 'I don't understand,' he would say, 'how a people like ours could have renounced the language of Kings and Prophets for a dialect that is, at best, alien.' People would try to argue with him. 'At the time of the Talmud, what language did the Jews use? Hebrew? No. Aramaic. And Maimonides, in what language did he write? Hebrew? No. Arabic. Then why not grant Yiddish the same status?' But he refused to listen. 'You compare yourself to Maimonides? To our Talmudic sages?' Whenever anyone touched upon this problem, the rationalist became irrational.

Mirele approached the table, leaned over Yoel, and glanced at the sheet of paper before him. 'Do you write your parents often?'

'Yes.'

She looked at him, mischief in her eyes. 'Tell me, do you ever utter more than three words at a time?'

'Yes. No. Sometimes.'

She burst into laughter. So did he.

'May I sit down?' Without waiting for his answer, she took a chair across from him.

'Are you always so shy?'

'Me? Shy?'

'No, someone who looks just like you.'

An odd sensation came over Yoel. His body felt awkward, cumbersome. If only he could rid himself of it. His head felt heavy, his eyes throbbed; his lips were cold.

'Speak to me,' said Mirele.

'About what?'

'About you. Your childhood. Your family. Your home.'

He tried but couldn't. She persisted, asking him specific questions. He answered in a faltering, breathless way. Then gradually it became easier. He spoke of his sisters and brothers. He spoke of his father the teacher. He spoke of his mother.

'You're smiling,' said Mirele.

'Am I?'

'You smile when you speak of your mother. I also smile when I recall mine. Even though I hardly knew her.'

Just then, Shlomo Reichmann put an end to their conversation. He burst in, beaming with joy.

'I found a letter, a priceless document,' he cried. 'It dates back to the early sixteenth century, to the time of King Alexander Jagiello. A Jewish merchant, P'tahya of Rhodes, wrote to him in 1504, thanking him for his decree authorizing Jews to participate in town fairs. He was somebody, this P'tahya. I also discovered two letters addressed to his rabbi concerning questions of ritual. He had a *mikvah* built for his own use. I have written proof of it. Not only that, he dared to sue a Christian for unfair competition and, strange as it may seem, he won.'

At this point, Mirele, who had been swept up by her father's excitement, asked a stream of questions, which he answered with considerable glee.

As for Yoel, he was still trying to regain his composure.

'Tell me, my young friend,' said Shlomo Reichmann, 'do you think your reticence is appropriate here? I bring you sensational news and there you are, sulking, as if we were on the eve of a fast! Do you have any idea what all this means? What would you say if I told you that with the help of these finds, I will be able to pinpoint the site where P'tahya lived?'

'Father,' said Mirele, 'Yoel is as excited as I am. You just don't know him yet. He is shy.'

'Well, well,' muttered her father. 'I guess you'll defend the whole world against me.'

'Not against you, Father. For you.'

It was an unforgettable evening for Yoel. He could not sleep all night, haunted as he was by the questions: How does one tell someone one loves that one loves her? Can one say it in Yiddish? And how does one say it without sounding foolish? If only there were someone he could ask for advice. But he could think of no one.

In the meantime, Mirele had invited him to accompany her to her 'cultural circle', a group that met several times a week to discuss political and cultural events. In spite of his shyness, Yoel found that he liked going there. First, because he felt drawn to the lively young people who were so passionate in their beliefs, and second, because each meeting brought him closer to Mirele. Did he realize that the group was only a cover for clandestine Communist activities? Knowing nothing about communism and its practices, he did not. Then again, Mirele had alluded to the fact that within the group was another more selective one that was not to be discussed. The Polish police had spies and informers everywhere. Prudence and vigilance were of the essence.

Anyway, the Communists in the group were safe as far as he was concerned. He didn't even know their names. All he knew was that they existed. He knew nothing about their leaders or their activities. He did not even know that Mirele was one of them.

She was. This he found out only after the Russians had arrived. At that time the group came out of hiding and some of its members obtained official posts. Mirele was attached to the office that dealt with Polish refugees. She was thus well placed to advise Yoel.

She did not mince her words: 'My comrades and I think it would be disastrous for you to return to Poland under Hitler.'

'What about my parents? My brothers and sisters?'

'You could do nothing for them there. Stay here and we'll try to bring them over.'

'You really think the Germans would let them out? And the Russians would let them in?'

'Look, Yoel, nothing is impossible. Besides, how do you know what our army can do? One day, it may push all the way to Rovidok, and we shall go along to liberate your family.'

Yoel gave in to her arguments. There were, of course, a few Jewish refugees who chose Hitler's hell over separation, but Yoel had faith in Mirele. They had become close. They were not officially engaged, but it was clear that they would marry. Shlomo Reichmann did not hide his satisfaction. One day he asked Yoel to join him on a walk through the city. As they made their way through the winding streets of Lvov, Shlomo gave his young protégé a tour of his favorite sites, saving the most important one for last. 'Look,' he said softly. 'This is the Synagogue of the Golden Rose. This is where Mirele's mother and I were married.'

Yoel stayed in Lvov. But he became increasingly distressed by the lack of news of his family, especially since so many frightening rumors were circulating. He often reproached himself for having left his parents, for not sharing their fate. After all, a Jew's place is with his people; a son's is with his parents. Hoping to raise his spirits, Mirele invited him to help with her father's community bulletin.

Under Soviet rule, Jewish life in Lvov had changed. On the one hand, there was now less reason to fear the anti-Semites. On the other, the new regime was suspicious of both the religious activities and the Zionist aspirations of the Jewish community. Of course, there were Jews among the soldiers and officers of the Red Army, as there were Jews in the ranks of the political police. But all told of nocturnal searches and arrests.

Said the optimists of Lvov, 'As long as we stay out of politics, everything will be all right.' Said the pessimists, 'In a Communist regime, not even the sun and the rain can stay out of politics.'

As for Shlomo Reichmann, he had faith in the future. Because of his daughter's standing with the Soviets? He chose to explain his optimism with an example from history.

'How can I forget that in 1648–49, during Chmielnicki's siege, the citizens of Lvov refused to hand over their Jewish neighbors? Oh, yes, I know. We have our anti-Semites and fanatics. But surely they are powerless in a Communist regime.'

Who could have guessed that the Communist regime would not last? Still, Mirele, 'Mirotchka' to the Soviets, must have had some inkling of it.

In mid-May, Shlomo Reichmann was rushed to the hospital for an appendectomy, leaving Mirele and Yoel alone in the house. Embracing that first night on Mirele's bed, they knew happiness. Through the open window, a spring breeze bore fragrances from faraway gardens.

Like lovers everywhere, Mirele couldn't help but ask, 'What are you thinking?'

'I'm searching.'

'For what?'

'For words.'

'What words?'

He smiled. 'I still don't know how to tell someone you love that you love her.'

'I can't believe it! I've never heard you make such a long speech!'

Kissing him, she whispered, 'It's easy. You just say it.'

'Then I will say it.' He took a deep breath:

'I will say what one says to someone . . .'

Mirele was laughing. 'What's the matter with you? Repeat after me: I love you.'

'I love you. There, I said it. Do you want me to repeat it?'

'Yes.'

That night when they made love, Yoel forgot his parents, Mirele her father. They thought only of their hunger for each other.

Then, shortly before dawn, they were seized by anguish. But neither spoke. As the new day broke, they saw one another in the faint light of dawn. Their eyes were filled with tears.

Not six weeks later they were separated. Their premonition had come true. On June 21, 1941, the war set the Russian-German borders ablaze. The cities fell with dizzying speed. As the Red Army retreated, it evacuated its personnel inland. 'Mirotchka' managed to obtain a seat for Yoel on one of the first trains heading east.

'What about you?'

'I'll follow soon. As soon as Father comes out of the hospital.' Shlomo Reichmann had had a relapse.

The day Mirele took Yoel to the station she was distraught. The station was crawling with soldiers and civilians. Pandemonium: yelling, running, weeping. Both struggled to hold back their tears.

'Are you sure you'll come soon?'

'I'm sure.'

'But how will we ever find one another?'

'All the convoys go to the same place. Soon, my father and I will be with you, I promise.'

As the train pulled into the station, the noise became deafening: the conductors, the policemen, the departing soldiers were all shouting.

'Hurry up,' urged Mirele, 'or you won't find a seat.'

'I don't want to leave without you.'

'Don't talk nonsense.'

She tried to laugh, to tease him, but failed. They kissed as though it were for the last time.

It was.

Shlomo Reichmann had been mistaken. The people of Lvov did not protect their Jewish neighbors. Quite the opposite: while the Germans were still outside the city, a bloody pogrom was organized against the Jews. Stefan Bandera and his men sacked their Houses of Prayer, plundered Jewish shops, smashed windows and doors, beat women and children. Their thirst for violence was insatiable.

Throughout the pogrom, Shlomo and Mirele hid in a cellar from which they witnessed the atrocities. In a worn notebook, Shlomo wrote down everything he saw and heard: 'They are smashing through the gate of old Dr Harzfeld's house . . . I see a young killer running, his face twisted by hate and greed. What treasures will he find in the home of the distinguished scientist? . . . I hear a woman scream, "No, no!" And the doctor's cries for help quickly stifled. I see, but I am ashamed to look, I am ashamed to live in these times, in this place . . .'

Mirele and her father were never evacuated. They remained in Lvov and died one autumn afternoon when the Germans decided that it was time to dispose of another thousand Jews.

As they walked toward death, she clutched his hand and whispered, 'I wonder where Yoel is at this moment.'

'I wonder too,' said Shlomo. 'Just as I wonder if anyone will wonder about us. If anyone will describe our march. This beautiful day. This serene sky. Will anyone tell of our mute prayers, our nameless sorrows? Will anyone tell how it all ended for the Jews of Lvov?'

'Father . . .'

'Yes?'

'How does one tell someone one loves that one loves him?'
'That's easy, Mirele. One tells him and one smiles.'
She smiled. 'I love you, Father.'

I don't want to, I don't want to go mad, Raphael says to himself. I don't want to rant and rave like Adam or Cain. I am Raphael, the father of a beautiful girl, the husband, the former husband, of a woman drawn to strength and incapable of understanding weakness. I am Pedro's friend.

You understand me, don't you, Pedro? I've been thinking and thinking, and here is what I've found: Madness is a question, not an answer. Madness lies not in the acceptance of time, but in the wish to alter it. Madness lies not in solitude but in the person confronting it. I don't mind entering it as long as it leaves me unharmed. I don't mind feeling the touch of death as long as I can turn away, run toward the sun and the sea. As long as I can raise myself toward God. What shall I do, Pedro? What distance separates man from God? What separates life from death? Madness from truth? And words from silence? I am free, and yet I am my own prisoner. So many years of searching and yearning, of false hopes, separate me from you, Pedro. Yet I still see you. I will go on seeing you, Pedro, as someone who revels in giving, who is willing to go to prison to set others free. No, I don't mourn you. Why live to mourn? Why create, since man too creates things that will die. The difference is that we do not create death, we do not create things so that they will die. The Talmud says, 'As long as I live, it behooves me to sanctify life, for neither life nor death is mine.' Then what is mine, Pedro?

It has been days, weeks, since I've come to this clinic, the only one of its kind in the world. I observe the patients, listen to them, speak to them, try to uncover their secrets. I must unmask the sick mind which, for reasons unknown, has lured me here to punish me. He wants to make me doubt you, to shake the foundation of my whole world. He wants me to doubt myself. Where is he hiding? Which shadow obscures his contorted face? He is my nemesis. For weeks and weeks he harassed me with his obscene nocturnal calls. You cannot imagine what he said about you, Pedro. Why does he loathe you so? And why does he torment me? Who is he? A patient? A doctor? A visitor, perhaps? When will he reveal himself to me?

To hell with him! To hell with all of them, Dr Benedictus included. I don't want their cheap benevolence. But how will I stay above water? Is it possible to swim without touching water? I'm going under, Pedro. You see, I sometimes follow the patients into their illness. Adam argues with God and it's as if my own life were at stake. On nights like these, when I speak to you, I also catch myself speaking to God. Like that poor devil Adam. Or Cain. Sometimes when he takes me for his brother I don't even protest. I answer him as if I were his brother. And then he screams, 'How dare you answer as if you were he? He is dead, I killed him. If you insist on trying to understand me, then make an effort to act as I would.' 'You're right,' I say, pretending to stay calm. 'Since your brother is dead, I must be you.' Because there is no one else. That is what assassin and victim have in common. Both are alone. Both are absolutely, irrevocably alone.

I rack my brain, Pedro. I need to understand what is happening to me. Since when have I been walking the edge of the abyss? Impossible to remember the exact moment: it eludes me. The breakup with Tiara tore me apart, but I went back to work, to teaching. She knocked me down, but I picked myself up and went on. As before. So when did I fall apart? Was it here, at the clinic? A frightening thought: What if this clinic was meant not to heal people but to make healthy people sick? This Benedictus: could he be a pervert, a criminal? If so, I'm lost. And so are you. Nobody will ever know the truth about you. Or that the truth about you, Pedro, was murdered right here in this wretched place.

And Karen, is she an accomplice? I wouldn't be surprised. As assistant to the director, she is suspect. But careful, I must not be hasty. Let's think it through: Who called me that first time? Who told me those terrible things about you, Pedro? Who suggested that if I wanted to know more, I had to come here without revealing the purpose of my visit? It was a man's voice, not a woman's. But that doesn't mean anything. They're all in this together. They're trying to tear me away from you and my memory of you. They're trying to destroy you. And drive me mad.

Pedro, my friend. We'll fight. We'll show them, won't we?

That's why I came here: to fight. To fight to the end. Your honor is at stake, Pedro. I know it and you know it. Our honor is at stake.

If only these patients would let me look inside them, let me see them without their masks. But they are determined to thwart me. They like the screen between us. In some cases, the screen is made of words; in others, it is made of silence.

'I don't want to, I don't want to speak,' says the 'prophet', who insists on being called just that. 'Don't try to force me. That won't work, not with me. So don't be a fool. Some prophets sing, others bless, still others curse. I am none of those. I am the prophet who chooses to be silent. And there is nothing you can do about it. My lips are sealed, and none of you has the right or the power to open them. Anyway, who is worthy of hearing the sound of my voice, the voice of my soul? Those who would hear me would not understand me, those who would understand me would not believe me. Better to remain silent. That is my secret, don't you see?'

Convinced that he has long curls in the manner of the ancient prophets, he shakes his head vigorously to emphasize a word here and there. Unfortunately, he is bald. And somewhat ridiculous as he stalks his room like a man possessed. He stops in front of a beautiful photograph of the Sinai desert. No doubt he sees himself in it.

He turns to Raphael and warns him:

'Neither this voice nor any part of me is mine. I am only a porter hired to carry someone else's baggage. Step aside, good man! You're young, you have many years of happiness before you. Don't jeopardize them.'

Raphael has the strange feeling that he's met this man before. He can predict every one of his gestures, every one of his outbursts. Still, this has little to do with real knowledge. It means only that he knows how to identify the mechanism that causes this patient to act or react. But that's all. He cannot see beyond. If Raphael were to take the prophet's place, even for a moment, he might be condemning himself to stay in it forever. And then, who would help him? Who?

He remembers how, as a philosophy student, he attended classes given by Charles Starkman, the illustrious professor of psychiatry at Bellevue. Twice a week, in the presence of his students, Starkman conversed with his patients as though they were guests in his living room. He talked to them about everything: weather, sports, current events. But for each, he set a trap.

An elegant woman, so elegant that she dusted her chair with her handkerchief every time she sat down, answered his questions with ease until the moment he 'inadvertently' uttered the word *ladder.* At that she went white and began trembling from head to toe. Other patients' thresholds were reached with a particular gesture, a touch or a glance. One patient would laugh uncontrollably, another would be racked with sobs. Raphael was appalled by the spectacle of Starkman's manipulation of these poor creatures. One day he asked him, 'How can you be sure that their truth does not lie precisely in their "madness"?' The professor answered without hesitation, 'Their truth, perhaps, but not ours.'

Which brings Raphael back to the nameless prophet's truth.

And his own. And the connection between the two. *I don't really understand it, Pedro, but in some mysterious way you are linked to this patient.*

I am here because of you.

I am here to fight your enemies. Did you know you have enemies? We all do. The world is full of them. That's how it is. As they say, that's life. Except that I'm against it. I don't accept life on those terms I won't let anyone denigrate your past. You may say it's all in the scheme of things. I reject such a scheme. In your name and in mine. After all, it was you who taught me that living can be as much a protest as dying. Do you remember, Pedro, when we walked in Paris, you told me that the path to enlightenment leads through the ravaged landscape of madness?

'Walk boldly down the street and dance,' you said. 'Dance on the burning road. Jump into the gutter of false pieties and established order. Shout yes, or no, call for order, any order, to come crashing down.'

'Only then,' you said, 'will our consciousness emerge victorious. A consciousness that calls for life rather than death. But Raphael, don't expect to live in a harmonious world, for the world is not that.'

I see you, Pedro. We were in Paris. I was young, very young. And you? Were you old? It doesn't matter now, it never did. What mattered was that you helped me to perceive the myriad reflections of the sea, the myriad sounds of the earth. You see, after all this time, I still hear your voice.

A bird began to sing and Ezra jumped: A bird in the ghetto? In winter? He threw down his hammer and rushed out of the workshop, into the street, to look for the bird.

For he was crazy, Ezra. Crazy about birds. Even back in Rovidok, everyone knew about his obsession with birds. He chased them, caught them, and set them free. He could spend hours nursing an injured bird. Not surprisingly, his father was displeased.

'At your age?' he said. 'At fifteen you're still running after birds? Aren't you ashamed?'

'No, Father. Forgive me, but I'm not ashamed of loving birds. God too loves them. Otherwise He wouldn't have created them.'

'I don't mind your loving them. But you are wasting too much time with them.'

'Forgive me, Father, but so is God,' replied Ezra.

Aharon suggested a compromise: three hours of study, four hours of carpentry, and one hour with the birds. Considering his passion for birds thus legitimized, Ezra accepted the conditions. With a slight change, however. He was with the birds only one hour a day, but they stayed with him much longer. Often, at the yeshiva or in the carpenter's shop, he was unable to concentrate because his thoughts were with his beloved friends. If only he could be as free as they, at home everywhere, with skies to explore and a nest to come back to. Though people made fun of Ezra, he was well liked. Always cheerful, always ready to help. Tall, strong, and amazingly handy, he could in a matter of minutes repair an oil lamp or a carriage wheel, build a toolbox, or hang a swing from a tree. He had golden hands, that was how they put it in Rovidok.

But his parents were not happy. They would have liked him to be a better student, to spend more time with books and less time with birds.

It was finally because of the birds that he had made the painful decision to leave Rovidok and take his chances in Lodz. His first job was with a weaver, his next in a dry-goods shop, then he worked in a furniture store. All his employers appreciated his diligence, his even temper, his kindness. His free time, especially Saturdays and Sundays, was devoted to his birds. To make sure they had shelter, he had built several nests in his courtyard. His neighbors referred to him affectionately as Ezra-the-Bird.

Is it possible? Ezra wondered on that bleak day in February. Did I really hear a bird sing? In winter? In the ghetto? My God, I must be losing my mind.

In the street, a passerby recognized him. 'So, Ezra? No birds today?'

'Don't worry, I'm looking for one.'

The man laughed. 'Go on, keep looking. If you find it, I'll come for dinner.'

Ezra returned to the workshop, disappointed. No trace of the bird. Yes, I am losing my mind, he thought.

Was this his punishment for having left his family? True, he had tried to go home. But it was not easy. Everything was happening so fast. The war. The total debacle. The railroad tracks had been bombed and travel was getting more hazardous by the hour. In any event, under the Germans one could not move freely. One needed all kinds of authorizations, each more difficult to obtain than the next. And they all cost money. And he had none. He had spent his last *zloty* on his birds. Furthermore, if he went back to Rovidok, what would happen to them? So Ezra allowed a few opportunities to slip by. And then it was too late.

On a practical level, he had little reason to complain. After meeting an assistant to Rumkowski, the Jewish 'king of the ghetto', he was assigned to head a department in a furniture workshop that supplied the military. His foreman was so proud of his skills that he would bring German officers to meet his exceptionally gifted worker. Foolishly, Ezra was flattered.

'You know what, Bilka?' he said one evening. 'Today a German officer was so pleased with my work that he gave me a cigarette.' Bilka was the young widow he had been renting lodgings from since the war. Mother of two children, a boy and a girl, she made her living cleaning houses. Ezra found her attractive. In her absence, he took care of the children, made toys for them, and taught them the names of the birds. They called him Uncle Ezra. At first that troubled him: 'I'm too young to be your uncle.' Then he got used to it, persuading himself that he was indeed their uncle. At night, a tired Bilka often showed her gratitude while the children slept peacefully in the kitchen. In February 1940, when the Baluty Quarter was officially designated as the ghetto, Ezra managed to find a room for the four of them. They were his family, after all.

Two hundred thousand Jews lived in the ghetto, but their number was decreasing steadily. Famine, sickness, exhaustion. Freezing days and nights. Proclamations, decrees, threats. The Jewish authorities kept repeating: 'Do your work, mind your own business, and you will survive.' Absurdly, in order to survive, the victims had to make their killers more powerful.

Productivity was the key word. One had to prove that one was productive, that one contributed to the enemy's war effort. For Ezra it was easy. Not so for Bilka. She had no trade. She could wash floors and do laundry, but her Jewish employers no longer had the means to pay for her services. With great difficulty, Bilka succeeded in finding work in a saddlery. Her children stayed home or played in the street. Like all ghetto children, they grew up fast. Their eyes told stories they were too small to understand.

One day, without warning, Bilka died. Oddly, she had not been sick. She had not complained of anything. What was this illness that had carried her off?

At the saddlery, they could give Ezra no logical explanation: 'Don't try to understand things that are incomprehensible.

You want to know what Bilka died of? It would be harder to understand if she had stayed alive. In the ghetto, it's easier to die than to live.'

Also:

'You want to know the truth? Bilka was lucky. She slipped from her chair and, just like that, she was dead. She literally slipped into death. Gently, very gently. She didn't have time to suffer.'

Also:

'Don't worry about her, she is no longer hungry. Or afraid. Or ashamed. I wish all of us a death like hers.'

She was buried without ceremony. Ezra and the children escorted her to the gate of the ghetto. It was raining. The children were shivering. To warm them up, he told them to run alongside him.

Looking troubled, the boy said, 'I'm afraid for Mother. She'll be cold.'

His sister corrected him. 'Don't be silly. Dead people don't feel the cold.'

During the weeks that followed, Ezra worked harder than usual. He took on extra jobs for the *Judenrat*. He worried about the children going hungry. And so he did not spare his strength to bring them bread and whatever else he could find. By now he had guessed what had happened to Bilka. She had fed her children with her own rations. She had sacrificed herself for them. He would do the same. And being stronger than she, he would hold out longer. To save the children: that had become his only purpose.

To protect them from the child hunters, the policemen whose task it was to arrest children for deportation, he had built an underground shelter in a remote outbuilding that belonged to the workshop.

'Don't be afraid,' he told them. 'You'll have plenty of air.

Nothing can block it. The important thing is not to make noise. Even if you're cold or hungry or if something hurts, don't make a sound. Our greatest enemy is noise. Do you understand?'

They understood. They endured hunger and cold; their legs, their arms, their eyes ached, but they remained silent. And they survived three lightning operations against the ghetto children.

But not the fourth. Ezra had not succeeded in sheltering them in time. They were out in the courtyard for a little air when the hunters arrived. He begged them to leave him the children. He promised them money, cigarettes, snuffboxes made of precious woods. When that didn't work, he threatened them. To no avail.

'These children are orphans and we have orders to pick up all orphans in the ghetto. If you try to interfere, you'll go to prison.'

'Fine, I'll go to prison. Only please don't take them away.'

He fought desperately, but was outnumbered. Three men kept him pinned to the ground, while a fourth led away the two children. Ezra screamed. The children never even opened their mouths. Instead, they attempted a smile as if to say, 'You see, Uncle Ezra? We're not making any noise.'

For the first time in his life, Ezra wanted to kill. To maim. To see blood flow. He wanted to smash everything in sight, destroy everything. The urge welled up inside him. From his bowels to his brain, it rumbled, roared, swept away all dams. He wanted to die; he wanted to kill himself and God. He wanted to become God so as to arrogate to himself the right to kill again and again. But he did nothing. He even stopped resisting. And when the hunters took their prey, he just sat on the ground staring after them. He never returned to the workshop. There was nothing more for him to do there.

At nightfall he found a way out of the ghetto, without false papers, without any help. He needed to go home. To see his mother, his father. To see his little brother Raphael, who was probably threatened by the same enemy. To protect him from the hunters.

Of course, Raphael at eleven was no longer a small child. But in Ezra's eyes he was. For him, all victims were birds, and all birds were children.

In a back office of the Moscow railroad station, drafting his personal report, Yoel knew that he had made a mistake. He should never have approached the Soviet officer. It had been a mistake to take the initiative. A mistake to try to influence his fate. And now it was too late.

He had acted impulsively, thinking that the authorities would expedite his reunion with 'Mirotchka' if informed of his relationship to her. Naive? Yes, Yoel was naive. In this, he resembled his father. Aharon too was naive. He had believed that education was everything; that if only you would take the trouble to explain, people would understand.

The tall young officer Yoel had accosted had been scrutinizing the passengers stepping off the train from Lvov. Most were making connections with trains headed for the interior. When Yoel told him that he had important information, the officer scrutinized him before responding, 'Fine, follow me.'

'Should I take my belongings?'

'No.'

Then:

'Maybe you'd better. You never know.'

He led him to a shabby, smoke-filled room where several officers were engaged in a heated debate. When their comrade walked in with Yoel, they stopped shouting.

'This citizen has some important information for us. Or so he says.'

'Very well,' said a captain, who seemed more jovial than his fellow officers. 'Come, sit here. Now take this paper and pencil and write.'

'Write . . . write what?' asked Yoel.

'Whatever it is you want us to know, just write it down.'

'What I have to tell you is simple, I . . .'

'Please, just write it down.'

His palms sweating, Yoel wrote: his fiancée, Mirele-Mirotchka Reichmann, was a devout Communist and held a high position with the military government in Lvov. She had remained in Lvov with her father, who was in the hospital. They were to arrive in Moscow at any moment, and he, Yoel, was waiting for them.

The captain scanned the sheet of paper, frowning. Then he handed him a second sheet. 'Now, tell us briefly who you are.'

Yoel wrote: Born in Rovidok, son of a schoolteacher, he had recently worked in Lvov. Separated from his family by the war, he was worried about them and was sad to be moving even farther away from them. But he so loved his fiancée that he would follow her to the ends of the earth. Rereading his words, he thought the last sentence too sentimental. He crossed out 'to the ends of the earth' and replaced it with 'to the Soviet Union.'

The captain read the second sheet, grunted, and showed it to the other officers. Their grunts were no more enlightening than his. After a brief discussion, the captain turned back to Yoel and said:

'What you are revealing to us is indeed of such importance that we have decided to take you to our superiors. They will see that your reunion takes place under the best possible circumstances.'

Was it because the captain had suddenly become too jovial? Or because the other officers had stopped their argument? Yoel had a premonition of impending doom, the feeling of having made a fatal error. He should never have stepped forward, spoken to a stranger, drawn attention to himself. Now it was too late.

Too late, he thought as he followed the captain to a black car. Too late, he told himself as they drove wordlessly through the crowded streets and squares. Too late, he reflected when the car came to a stop in front of a vast, windowless building.

One hour later – can such hours be measured in minutes? – Yoel had become unrecognizable to himself. Suddenly cut off from all points of reference, his universe had become unreal. Was it really he, Yoel, the schoolteacher's son, who was passing through the prison gates? Being put behind bars? Being pushed down endless corridors by a foul-smelling guard?

Once upon a time, in another era, before the war, his father had told him of a man possessed by a dybbuk, the wandering soul of a dead person in search of reparation. It's happening to me, thought Yoel. I am home in Rovidok and I think that I am in a Soviet prison. *I* think? No, the dybbuk thinks. It is he, the dybbuk, who is the prisoner. It is he who is stopping before a cell. It is he who staggers as he enters, almost falling to the ground. He and not I. Of course. What would I be doing in prison? I have done nothing wrong.

'Why are you here?' asked a voice.

Yoel almost answered, 'I'm not here. Someone else is here. A dybbuk has taken my place.'

Instead he said, 'I don't know.'

'Where do you come from?'

'Lvov.'

Another voice:

'Were there many arrests in Lvov?'

'I don't know.'

That was the truth: he knew nothing. He didn't even know whether he had heard the question right. Still in shock, he observed himself move as in a dream he had strayed into by chance.

'You'll sleep over here,' somebody said. 'Near the door. Your place is waiting for you. Sorry about the stench.'

Yoel tried to see where he was but the darkness refused to give way. Somebody pulled him to the right and ordered him to sit down. He obeyed mechanically.

'Where am I?' he asked weakly.

'The Butyrka.'

'What's that?'

'A resort hotel.'

When the laughter subsided, the others questioned him further about the outside world. Lvov, what was it like under the Soviet occupation? What was the food situation, and what were people in Lvov saying about the war? Yoel answered as best he could. But what came out was unintelligible. Stopping in mid-sentence, choking on his words, he apologized again and again for his incoherence.

'It's okay, don't worry,' somebody said. 'Your reaction is normal for a newcomer. You'll get used to it, you'll see.'

He leaned back against the damp wall. The smell of the latrine was making him sick. Eyes shut, he tried to calm his breathing. And to organize his thoughts. Suddenly, Mirele appeared before him: laughing, graceful, wearing her pink gauze dress.

Aren't you hot? she asks. Yes, he is hot, he is suffocating. I'm not, says Mirele. But I'm thirsty. Me too, says Yoel. A glass of cold water, get me a glass of cold water. Of course, she says. I'll get it for you. Yoel is panic-stricken: No, no, don't go away, don't leave me alone! You're afraid I won't come back? asks

Mirele, stroking his hair. Yes, Mirele, I'm afraid. How silly you are, she says. Then she disappears. He goes looking for her, he must find her. Mirele, where are you? Where is my Mirotchka? I love you, I love you, I'll find the words to say it, you'll see. Just stay with me.

A strong grip and a gruff voice tear him away from his love.

'Hey, you, I asked you your name!'

'Yoel,' he said. 'Yoel Aharonovitch Lipkin.'

'What did you do for a living?'

'I worked in a bookshop.'

'You sold books?'

'Yes, we sold books.'

'What kind of books? Schoolbooks?'

'All kinds.'

'And you were allowed to sell whatever you wanted? Even foreign novels? Zola and Goethe?'

'No, I was talking about before. After, we closed the shop.'

'And then what did you do?'

'I worked at the cultural center.'

'You don't mean cultural. You mean propaganda.'

Yoel shook his head. 'No, I mean cultural.'

The gruff voice sounded weary. 'If that's what you want to call it, go ahead.'

Somewhere a door clanged shut and abruptly they all fell silent. And went to sleep. Except for Yoel. Despite the fatigue from the journey, despite the shock, he lay awake. Squinting in the dark, he counted a dozen people or so. Two or three slept on cots, the rest were sprawled all over the floor. They snored, whistled in their sleep, thrashed about. From time to time somebody went Shshsh! And all noise ceased. I'm having a nightmare, thought Yoel. I'm being punished. I should never have left Mirele. I should never have abandoned Shlomo. I should never have forsaken my parents. My poor parents:

where are they now? What are they doing? What are the Germans doing to them? It's my fault, Yoel told himself, it's all my fault. I should never have left Rovidok. If I were at home, I could protect you . . . He did not fall asleep until moments before dawn. When the morning call came, he lay there spent.

The dusty daylight filtering through the barred window gave him his first clear view of his cellmates. Lined, unshaven faces, swollen lips, feverish eyes. Do I look like that? he wondered. They were given water, crusts of bread. Yoel could not swallow.

'Try,' said a redheaded man sitting across from him. 'You must eat. You'll need your strength.'

'I can't,' said Yoel.

'You'd better learn.'

The redhead, whose name was Sergei, was in charge. It was he who 'welcomed' new inmates, assigned space, and settled disputes. All by virtue of his seniority. A high official in the Caucasus in the days of Yezhov, he had been in this cell for more than two years. A Party member since childhood, Sergei had remained a Communist even in prison. 'The secret police make mistakes,' he said. 'All that proves is that their chiefs are incompetent. From there to conclude that the Communist idea is false, is a step only an Enemy of the State would take.' Feigned loyalty, perhaps? Yoel never found out. In prison, everybody hides something. You never know if the thief is an informer, or if the professor is an agent. In Yoel's cell there were three thieves, two embezzlers, several 'Enemies of the State.' And what about me, what am I? Yoel wondered. Why did they arrest me?

'What matters,' Sergei told him, 'is not to give up. Not to become resigned. Or bitter. Bitterness is the worst of all evils. You will suffer as I have suffered, a little more, a little less.

What matters is not to let yourself rot inside. That is what bitterness is: internal decay.'

Sergei had adopted a paternal attitude toward his youngest cellmate.

'Don't listen to him,' said Yefrem, an intellectual who preferred to be called a thief rather than a subversive. 'You want to survive? Learn to steal. Where I come from, everybody steals. My town would not survive if its people did not steal. True, you risk prison. But if you don't steal, you also risk prison. So, what difference does it make?'

The talk was of *ukases, dielo,* and Paragraph 58. To confess or deny? Give them what they wanted or let them fight for every word? Sergei, on the strength of his considerable experience, advised his new protégé not to resist the interrogators:

'I resisted and I'm sorry I did. The interrogations went on for weeks. Night after night. I thought I would go mad. My advice to you: don't play tough. They'll tell you that you tried to sabotage the Kremlin. Sign, even if you never set foot in Moscow. They'll tell you that you tried to corrupt your wife's brother. Sign, even if you're not married. They'll tell you that you personally jeopardized the security of the Soviet Union. Sign. Sign right away, because one way or another, you'll end up signing.'

'But I am innocent,' protested Yoel.

'That's beside the point,' said Sergei.

Yoel braced himself for the first interrogation. Uncertainty. Fear. Fear of suffering. Fear of the unknown. Fear of death. Even though that was one possibility his mind rejected categorically: 'Die, me? At my age? So far away from my family?' He could not envision it.

Looking for help, he conjured up his father's image. Aharon, with his gentle gaze, where could he be at this moment? He imagined him sitting at the table, reading aloud a passage from the Bible, patiently explaining it to his pupils. 'Stay with me, Father. Soon I shall be called. I shall face the prosecutor alone. I'm afraid to be alone.' But his father, absorbed in his reading, did not hear him. Then Yoel went into the kitchen. 'Mother, you never refused me anything. Don't refuse me now. I need your presence beside me. I know I should not impose my misery on you, but if you're with me, I will not suffer as much.' Busy with the Shabbat meal, she did not hear him either. Yoel went out into the yard and saw his brother Raphael climbing a cherry tree. 'You, Raphael, you'll come with me, won't you?' And Raphael smiled. 'Of course, Yoel. Call me and I'll be there with you.'

But the interrogation was slow in coming.

'Maybe they have forgotten me,' said Yoel.

'Never,' declared Sergei. 'People outside may forget you, but not these people.'

That night, two 'Enemies of the State' were taken away for interrogation. One was brought back in the morning in a daze. The other never reappeared. 'What is the significance of the one's return and the other's disappearance?' asked Yoel.

'There is none,' said Sergei. 'No prisoner ever understands a prosecutor. The prosecutor's logic is different from ours. One man confesses and he comes back, another man confesses and he is sent away. The opposite is also true: one man denies everything and he is sent away; his friend denies everything and he comes back. There is no rule.'

The prisoner who had just been brought back overheard this exchange but did not react. Who knows what he had to endure? thought Yoel. And then: Who knows what I'll have to endure?

Two nights later he found out. The door slid open and a guard appeared, a sheet of paper in his hand:

'All those whose names begin with *L*, stand up.'

This is it, thought Yoel, pulling himself up with great difficulty; he had trouble steadying himself.

'Your name?'

'Yoel Aharonovitch Lipkin.'

'Come with me, Prisoner Lipkin. Hurry up!'

It was silly, but at that moment Yoel had only one regret: that he had drunk too much water. What an idiot I am, he thought as he left his cell. I should have emptied my bladder. The word *emptied* became central to his thoughts. His head felt empty, his memory empty. Where had he come from? Where was he going? His past was erased. All he knew was that he had to walk in front of the guard, set one foot before the other, look straight ahead and . . . He went through door after door, corridor after corridor, became saturated with the silences around him, and finally received the order to halt in front of a grimy steel door. The guard knocked and it opened from the inside. Yoel was shoved into a large room flooded with naked light.

'Step forward,' said a harsh voice.

Yoel obeyed, advancing cautiously. A cluttered table, a man bent over it, writing. Yoel could not stop blinking. He didn't know that light could stick to the skin and burn.

'Stand up straight.'

The same harsh voice. Again Yoel obeyed. Teeth clenched, eyes staring ahead, he held his body erect. How long would he have to stand like this? Already his right leg was numb. A thousand needles were pricking his ankle. His neck was so stiff it felt like an object. Then there was his bladder. And his panic. If only I could sleep, Yoel thought.

'You're not here to sleep.'

If only I could sleep with my eyes open. Go away from here. To Mirele. The train, Mirele. It's leaving. Let it leave, I'm staying with you. Come, let's go home . . .

'And you're not here to dream.'

. . . Let's go home, Mirele. I'll tell you how much I love you. See, I know how to say it. Look, Mirele: My father is smiling. Have you ever seen such a smile? God Himself must envy him this smile.

'Prisoner Lipkin, do you understand?'

How vast the space that separates one word from the other. One can fill it with a thousand images, a thousand dreams. How vast the chasm between two words. I fill it and I'm off on a journey to Lvov and from there on to Rovidok. Here I am, back at the Butyrka, and the voice has not spoken again.

'Name, first name, and patronym.'

In a shrill, unrecognizable voice, Yoel answered, 'Lipkin, Yoel Aharonovitch.'

Still standing stiffly, he felt his body becoming heavier by the second. Just let him go on with the interrogation, Yoel thought. Soon I'll be able to detach my mind from my body. I have to: my body is my enemy.

'Who sent you?'

'The guard. He's the one who . . .'

'Idiot!'

Blinded by light and pain, Yoel had only a blurred view of the figure in front of him. The man had raised his head. He was no longer writing.

'Who sent you to Moscow?'

'Nobody.'

'But you are, in fact, in Moscow. Who sent you?'

'Nobody, but . . .'

Everything was mixed up in Yoel's head. Mirele, her sick father, the evacuation, the train. The train is leaving. Don't leave. Stop . . .

'The Germans . . .'

'The Germans sent you, is that it?'

'No.'

'They sent you to spy.'

'No.'

Sergei's advice: Sign, sign anything. No. Yoel will not sign. He, a spy? A Jew like himself, a German spy against the Soviet Union? Preposterous. He felt like shouting in anger and disgust.

Instead, he collapsed.

How long did he remain unconscious? Someone was pouring cold water on his face. He awoke to find himself in the same place, in front of the table, seared by the same mass of light. Facing the same interrogator. Who was asking the same questions:

'Who sent you here to spy on us?'

Yoel gave the same answers:

'Nobody. Nobody sent me. Nobody.'

The man stood up. Though no taller than Yoel, he dominated the room.

'You're lying,' he shouted.

Now he stood two inches from Yoel:

'Your confession states that your parents are in occupied Poland, and your fiancée is in Lvov. And you just happened to come to Moscow. Are you telling me that's normal?'

Yoel received his words like so many lashes. He bit his lips until they bled. The prosecutor was right. No, it was not normal that he should be in Moscow while his parents remained in Poland; it was not normal that he should be in Moscow while Mirele left the Lvov railroad station to go home, alone.

'You're a traitor,' roared the prosecutor.

Traitor, traitor – the word reverberated in Yoel's head. Yes, I betrayed my parents; I betrayed my brothers, my sisters; I betrayed the person I love most in the world.

'Whom are you working for? Who sent you?'

Yoel could only shake his head from right to left, from left to right. What was he trying to say? No, no, I'm not who you think I am, I'm not what you think I am, I'm not saying what you hear, I'm not seeing what you see, I no longer see anything, I no longer think anything, I no longer am anything.

Again he fainted. When he came to, he was in another cell. Sergei? No more Sergei. No more thieves, no more 'Enemies of the State.' He was alone. A guard was reading him the regulations: forbidden to sleep, forbidden to sit, forbidden to speak, that is, forbidden to speak to oneself. They will succeed in breaking me, thought Yoel. I am beginning to accept their logic. In a way, I already have: of course my behavior is suspect. It is a fact that I came alone. Why? That's a good question. Yes, I did leave Lvov to escape the Germans. I left Lvov without Mirele because that was how she wanted it. Why had she wanted it like that? I could have waited another day, another week. She wanted me to leave without her. Why? Here I go, suspecting *her* now . . . Madness, I know. I am going mad.

While pacing his new cell, Yoel went over and over the prosecutor's questions, and his own answers. Should he have 'confessed'? Would he have the strength to go on denying the charges during the interrogations to come? Starved, exhausted, he was led to the prosecutor, muttering, 'No, no, nobody, nobody.' He was convinced that his only hope lay in this limited vocabulary. Any departure from it would mean catastrophe, not only for himself but also for Mirele. Since it was she who had sent him, she would be held responsible for his 'criminal' activities against the State.

After the twelfth session, he felt that he was reaching his limit. The waiting, the blinding light, the interminable questions, the provocations – he could not go on. He thought: they are winning.

Suddenly, he had a vision of himself as mad. And he

thought: since they want me to go mad, I'll oblige them. I'll say anything that comes to my mind. Perhaps then they'll leave me alone.

'I confess,' he announced at the next session. 'I did not come of my own free will. God forced my hand. I am His emissary. And I am here to tell you the truth, the eternal and fiery truth from the very mouth of the Almighty: the end of time is approaching. Whosoever will have the courage to save my people, that man I shall bless.'

The prosecutor was stunned. A long moment elapsed before he regained his composure: 'What are you babbling about? Are you mocking me?'

'I am God's emissary and God is not in the habit of mocking people.'

Yoel was searching for a name, a voice, an identity among the prophets of Judea who had peopled his childhood. Amos or Habakkuk? Isaiah or Jeremiah? He opted for Jeremiah:

'I left the Holy Land, my family, and my friends to go into exile. I am a messenger of God, and I have come to tell you that your survival depends on that of my people. I have come to tell you that there will be a fire . . .'

The prosecutor let him speak without interrupting him. Carried by his imagination, Yoel plucked whole passages from the ancient prophetic texts. The warning to Babylonia and Chaldea, the forces of the South and of the North, the interdictions against adultery and idolatry. He spoke and spoke, jumping from subject to subject, from book to book, from era to era. The prosecutor was transfixed. Only when Yoel seemed out of breath did the prosecutor ring for the guard to take the prisoner back to his cell.

'He is sick. Let him rest until tomorrow.'

From that night on, the same scene was repeated many times. As Jeremiah, Yoel spoke and spoke, every word carrying him far, very far. Away from Moscow, away from this prison, away from his fear . . .

He saw himself at thirteen, celebrating his *bar mitzvah*. At the House of Study, surrounded by the congregation, he was reciting the *Haftarah,* which, that particular week, was taken from the Book of Jeremiah. As he chanted the text in the presence of his father and his masters, he remembered what his father had told him the night before: 'When a Jewish boy recites Jeremiah, he is Jeremiah.' And Yoel was Jeremiah. As Jeremiah, every morning he left Anatoth to go up to Jerusalem, to preach the Divine Word. As Jeremiah, he went to see King Zedekiah to implore him not to venture into a war against the Babylonians. As Jeremiah, he was present at the destruction of Jerusalem and the plunder of its Temple. Thus, one could pray in Rovidok and imagine oneself in Judea. One could be a young Jewish boy in Poland and wander through the hills surrounding the City of David. One could, in one's dreams, build other dreams in which every word serves as a shelter for the Word of God.

'And God said to Jeremiah: Go and be my messenger to the multitudes in Russia. You shall be called a spy. You shall be accused of treason. Don't heed the slanderers, their hate will turn them against themselves.'

Comfortably ensconced in his new role, Yoel perfected it from one session to the next. His voice would alternately threaten or beseech. His vision of the future would be bleak or reassuring, according to his mood. He acted on an invisible stage before an audience of one; and he knew that his life or death hinged on the quality of his performance. Sometimes he made an effort to remain lucid, at other times he drove himself into a frenzy. Then, the room would spin around him. As would his words. As would his memories.

One night the prosecutor brought in a psychiatrist to examine him. Yoel managed to sidestep his traps.

'Interesting case,' said the doctor. 'Of course, this may be a temporary condition. Let's give him some time.'

Yoel was right. Madmen are left in peace.

For one year, they left him alone.

'It's all my fault,' whispers the old man called Abraham. 'I should have been more realistic, less gullible. I should have been a better judge of man's nature. His baseness runs deeper than his goodness or even his thirst for goodness. Men are savages, animals. Only animals don't make a pretense of generosity. I should have understood that in a society ruled by man, instinct triumphs over reason. Man is evil, I should have known that. Envious, greedy, petty, he is driven to possess what is not his. He is determined to dominate, to humiliate. Truth? Dignity? He couldn't care less.'

Abraham's face radiates goodness. He speaks deliberately, weighing every word. At regular intervals he examines his hands. Only reluctantly does he look up at the person he is addressing.

'Please don't judge me,' he says quietly. 'I do enough of that myself. You see, I once had a son, a boy to whom I wanted to pass down the lessons I had learned at his age. He was twenty, my son, and he had his whole death before him . . .'

Sitting in the patient's room, Raphael observes him obliquely so as not to offend him. To look busy, he plays with his handkerchief, his pen. Raphael finds the man appealing; he senses in him a kindred solitude.

'They call me Abraham,' the patient says softly. 'Like the patriarch. In fact, I am the patriarch.'

Raphael is not surprised by his remark; he almost anticipated it. Abraham has a timeless quality. Of all the patients he has met thus far, Abraham seems the most genuine.

'One day I said to God: "You don't need me anymore. Let me go back to earth. Your children, who are also mine, are living through difficult times. I may be of some service to them." And God yielded to my argument. Even though He had some of his own and they were strong, very strong. For instance, that the laws of nature must not be violated. That the dead belong to the dead. That God, and God alone, can reconcile life and death. "And what about the prophet Elijah?" I countered. "Does he not go back and forth between heaven and earth, feeling at home everywhere?" "No," said God, "he is in exile everywhere. Is that what you want?" "I accept exile," I answered. "For my sons are in exile." Whereupon God smiled. "Are you really going to abandon me for human beings too weak to resist temptation?" "Of course not," I answered. "You know very well that I shall never abandon you. I shall always stay at your side. Anyway, I know you, you don't fool me: you're not as strict as you seem. You are quick to threaten, but with rare exceptions, you are merciful. And when man suffers for you, you suffer with him. When I leave heaven, I'll find you again on earth. You know it and so do I."'

He gets up, takes a few steps. Suddenly Raphael is transported back to his childhood. His father used to frown like that, walk like that, hands behind his back, whenever he was trying to defeat anxiety. Raphael sees him in the distance, at the edge of dusk.

The patient stops in front of the window. 'To be truthful, it is God I sought in my wanderings,' he says. 'I knew the Creator could be found inside His creation. Particularly whenever Creation went awry. A child cries in the night? It is He who collects its tears. An old man trembles at dawn? It is He who soothes him. A mother faces her hungry child? It is He who gives her strength. I can attest to it, for I have seen Him at work. I saw Him intervene in Babylon, in Persia, in Spain . . . In my role of patriarch, I was present whenever and wherever the Children of Israel endured humiliation, plunder, and massacre. One day I shall describe to you the events at Blois, Mainz, and Rhodes.'

Raphael feels like saying, Why wait? Tell me now, immediately. You never know when another opportunity will arise. But he is too awed by the depth of the man's vision to interrupt. Let him set the pace of their conversation; let him lead the way.

'Now I would rather tell you about my son, his life and his death,' says the patient after a long silence. 'It's my own fault that I lost him. I wanted to educate him, make him into a good Jew. We were living in a small village, not far from Zhitomir. Since there was no Jewish school – the entire system was Communist – I became his tutor. At three, my son knew the basic prayers; at five, he read the Bible; at eight, we studied together, with the fervor of persecuted disciples, the varied and dazzling Treaties of the Talmud. I was proud of him, proud of us. Sometimes at night I would evoke the memory of my wife: if only she could see us now. I would speak of her to my son. He would listen with all his being, without ever saying a word. When I asked him if he had an image of his mother, he answered, "Yes, I see my mother in every gentle and beautiful woman."'

The patient is just as Raphael had imagined Abraham: strong, determined, yet kind. Suddenly he finds himself believing the old man's tale. This is no longer a raving patient, but the patriarch himself.

'During the occupation, I found a shelter for the two of us. As the days and nights flowed into a bottomless well, my son and I found refuge in words. A peasant brought us bread and water. I asked him, "Why are you doing this? Why are you risking your life for Jews?" "Because you are the last," he answered. Through him, we were kept informed of events in the outside world. The front advanced, retreated, the mass graves filled with corpses, the sky set fire to the earth, death enlarged its kingdom, evil sowed its seed unchecked, and all that time my son and I continued to study the ancient texts in which God is God and life is sacred.

'One evening – or was it morning? – the peasant said to me, "I don't understand you, neighbor. You have a son, you love him, and you want him to live. Why don't you teach him to survive?" "But I do," I answered him, startled. "How do you think my people survived exile if not through study?" And, like a fool, I began explaining to him Jewish faith in the Word. Forgetting that I was speaking to an illiterate peasant, I quoted to him the Hasidic commentary on Noah. When God ordered him to build an ark, he used the word *teva,* which in Hebrew means both *ark* and *word*. "It is by building words that you will survive the flood." The peasant was not convinced. Shaking his head he said, "You're a strange man, neighbor. You should be teaching your son to run faster than the hare at the first sign of danger. You should be teaching him to live on fruit and herbs. But what you *must* teach him is to pass for a Christian. The enemy is cruel, death is ready to pounce, and here you are, occupying yourself with things that have nothing to do with staying alive." "You don't understand," I answered, "you cannot understand. What rain is to you, the Word is to us. It nurtures our lives; without it we'd wither like wheat in a drought." Still shaking his head, the peasant started toward the secret opening of the hiding place. Suddenly, he stopped. "Tell me, neighbor, there is something I don't understand: you say that you owe your survival and your son's to your 'word'. And all this time I thought you owed it to me . . ."

'I don't remember why I wanted to convince the peasant, but I did. "Listen, my friend," I said. "Please try to understand: the Word is everything. Through the Word we elevate ourselves or debase ourselves. It is refuge for the man in exile, and exile for the righteous. How would we pray without it? How would we live without it? Don't underestimate the Word, my friend. Don't fight the Word. Let it possess you and in return you will receive life's most generous offering: the impulse that brings man closer to God."

'The peasant was clearly amazed by my discourse, but he soon recovered. "God? Whose God? Yours? Who is protecting you from the Germans? He or I? It is *my* 'word' you should be teaching your son. Do you hear me? *My* 'word', not His!" In spite of the darkness, he must have seen the expression on my face, for he began to laugh. "No hard feelings, neighbor. You know I want to help you. I look at the two of you who are both in mortal danger. Hundreds of your kind are in mass graves, don't you know that? Your son must learn to outwit the enemy, and that he can't do with your 'word'. Teach him to drink the morning dew, to sleep with the cows, with the wolves if necessary; teach him to survive in the forest, teach him to live, for heaven's sake. Otherwise, I promise nothing!" I was about to reply when he turned and left. And I, blind, stupid, or both, said to my son, "I feel sorry for him; he is a good man but he does not understand." And we went back to our text.

'But the Word did not save us. We were denounced, arrested, and imprisoned. In our cell there were other Jews, fugitives from the surrounding villages, who had also been hiding in the forest. Some of them ran away; they knew how. My son did not. They knew how to climb walls, jump fences, live in the woods. My son did not. They could find their way on the path to survival. My son only knew his way through books, and the songs of days gone by, and the wisdom of our sages. Against the enemy he was defenseless. And it was all my fault. Who will forgive me? Who will forgive Abraham the death of his son?'

The patient is on the verge of tears. Raphael would like to console him, to say to him, 'Abraham, Abraham, come down from Mount Moriah; you will see your son again, he is waiting for you below. Your son has not spoken, and that is good. His silence is your Word.'

That is what Raphael would like to say, but there is such despair in the patient's eyes that he is afraid to speak. Just as he is afraid to remain silent.

When Raphael arrived at the clinic, he had no idea of the complexity of the world he was locking himself into. Days, weeks, were passing and he was no closer to his goal: to identify the caller who could shed light on Pedro's activities since they were separated. He was, after all, Raphael's only hope of ever finding Pedro again.

Raphael came to the clinic to find the caller. He stayed on out of fascination with the patients. They intrigue him as much as their treatment. Not being a psychiatrist, he is in no position to judge the therapeutic value of Dr Benedictus's methods. He wonders what percentage of the patients are cured. And how long they usually stay.

One day he broaches the subject with Benedictus. 'How do you know when a patient has recovered?'

'He knows it before I do,' answers the director.

'And he tells you?'

'No.'

'Why not?'

'Because the idea of recovery is terrifying. Socrates fears leaving Socrates, you know.'

Yes, Raphael knows. He too is afraid of leaving. He has

become strangely attached to this clinic where fragile beings live out their distorted dreams. He wishes he could reach these poor creatures, draw them out of their isolation.

How bizarre, thinks Raphael, to seek salvation in a psychiatric clinic. Then again, why not? Who says that madmen cannot help the 'sane'? Often their madness consists precisely in their wish to save others. Raphael has met his share of madmen. He owes them some of his most exalted moments.

Long ago, in Rovidok, the old madman with veiled eyes persuaded him that it was possible for one man to die in another man's place, and that divine redemption depends upon human redemption.

Later, in Paris, another madman had helped him discover the triumphs and failures concealed within words.

And then, in the Far East, yet another madman had taught him the rewards of silence, and later, the rewards beyond silence.

Of course, Pedro too had been a madman in his own way. He was forever telling Raphael that one must not seek to understand, that one must understand without seeking, that it is sometimes necessary to seek in order not to understand.

At the clinic, Raphael is seeking. His free hours are spent in the library, where many of his favorite works are close at hand: Philo of Alexandria and Maimonides, Saint Augustine and Luther, Spinoza, Erasmus and Don Itzhak Abrabanel. There are old and new editions, which he has spent countless hours rearranging. There are classic and not-so-classic interpretations of the failed sacrifice of Isaac, the solitary death of Moses, the abandonment of King Saul. Raphael loves the dark-paneled reading room, which reminds him of the book-filled dining room back home.

On Friday afternoons, Aharon would gather his sons around him and chant the *Sidrah*, the Torah reading of the week.

Sometimes they would also read the translation by Onkelos-the-Convert. According to the Talmud, Onkelos, who was a nephew of the Roman emperor, was asked, 'Why do you wish to give up the faith of your forefathers and the life they have prepared you for?' And Onkelos answered, 'I feel irresistibly drawn to the Jewish people.' 'The Jewish people?' exclaimed his uncle. 'Don't you know its fate: punishment and humiliation?' 'Yes, I know.' 'Then why do you wish to share it?' 'Because,' said Onkelos, 'the Jewish people is the only one whose children study the secret of Creation . . .'

Aharon and his sons would also read the poetic Biblical translation by Yonathan son of Uziel, another convert to Judaism. It is said that when Yonathan studied the Torah, a celestial fire, the fire of Sinai, encircled him, scorching the wings of birds flying past.

Surely, Onkelos, Yonathan, and the Talmud, with its Greek influences, had awakened in Raphael a passion for ancient literature. Still, what would his father say if he could see him in this library used solely by madmen and their therapists?

During weekly psychodramas, which Dr Benedictus holds in the reading room, Raphael looks on as some patients howl, others withdraw into themselves. Raphael is reminded of Dr Starkman's classes at Bellevue. The scenes unfolding here are as disturbing. He again feels like a voyeur. The first time he watches, his thoughts drift to Pedro. Could his caller be hiding behind the mask of a patient? But soon he is drawn into the game.

There are days when the clinic seems like paradise. A paradise in which God rules firmly but mercifully. The staff? Would-be angels, trained to bring peace to the battle-weary, to all those betrayed by their own will or lack of it, to all those who suffer from the absence of peace.

Of course, he can leave at any time. He can go home, prepare his courses, invite Rachel to spend a few days with him at the beach. But he has a purpose. And that purpose has not yet been accomplished. Would it ever be? What if, somewhere along the way, he were to abandon it? What if, with time, he were to forget all about Pedro, his name, his face? Though Raphael had known madmen as a boy, it was not until he came to the clinic that he discovered madness could be contagious.

And what if he were to stay on indefinitely? His colleagues would adjust to his absence soon enough. So would his students. Tiara, his former wife, would continue not to think about him: What does she care whether he is in an ashram in India or adrift on the Amazon? She has remarried. It is a happy marriage, or so it seems. What about Rachel? Little Rachel. Well, not so little. She is fifteen. Raphael's heart aches just thinking about her. Is she happy? Sad? Does she miss him? Probably not. The proof? She lives with her mother. Still, that had been the court's decision, not hers. Rachel, poor little Rachel. He had spent whole nights watching her sleep, he had spent long hours waiting for a smile. And now? Is she happy? What a dangerous concept that is, one that encourages expectations that can never be met. It's thanks to that concept that Tiara left him.

Raphael is not ashamed to admit that he had loved his wife; that, in truth, he still loves her. He loved her keen mind, her mischievous ways, her disquieting beauty. And he accepted her hostile silences, her irrationality, her tantrums.

And she, what had she loved about him? She said . . . But she said so many things even when she said nothing. Perhaps she loved his love for her. No matter. It is over.

And Rachel in all this? If he decides to stay at the clinic, will she know how to reach him? Rachel, little, not so little, Rachel, who is surely looking for someone, but almost as surely, not for her father.

*

A memory:

A Fifth Avenue bookshop. Raphael was leafing through translations: Hesse, Mann, Kafka. A new translation so absorbed him that he was oblivious of someone having bumped into him until he heard the words, 'Excuse me.' He looked up. A woman was smiling teasingly, provocatively. 'I didn't know that literature could be an anesthetic.' He blushed. Women always made him blush, even when they were not really beautiful, like this one. Totally beautiful, desperately beautiful. Raphael was struck dumb. And the beautiful woman with the long dark hair would not budge. She stood there and mercilessly sized him up. If only he could have turned on his heel, walked away, but he could not. His legs refused to obey him. For God's sake, what did she want from him? Her voice seemed to come from another realm: 'Now that I think of it, what good is literature anyway?' He vaguely knew that he should be answering her, trying to dazzle her with witty conversation, making her laugh. He should be suggesting that they have coffee and then . . . leave things to the god of all students in love.

But his shyness won out. As always. He closed the book, mumbled some foolishness, and rushed out the door, trembling with rage and shame, berating himself for his shyness. That day Raphael loathed himself. He was unable to concentrate. He blamed himself for being unworldly. He made coffee but could not swallow, he lit a cigarette and stubbed it out. He lay down but sleep refused to come. He began to curse this strange woman who had nothing better to do than to insinuate herself into his life, to unsettle him, now and forever. He decided to return to the bookshop tomorrow. If she dared to be there, he'd settle his score with her. If she didn't come, well, that was her loss.

The next day, at the same hour, he went to the bookshop

and stationed himself in front of the same counter to look over, or try to look over, the very same works. The minutes went by, an hour. His body was tense. She would not come, he was sure of it, he was ready to bet anything she would not come. She would go anywhere, harass anyone, but today was one day she would not appear in this bookshop. And he was right: she did not show up.

Raphael walked out into the brilliant sunshine, but he was in no mood to appreciate it. He heard and saw nothing. Not the gridlocked traffic and blaring horns, not the peddlers hawking their wares, not the crowds racing toward the subway entrances; he was nearly trampled. Oblivious of the street preachers trying to engage passersby in their discourse, oblivious of the Hasidim on Forty-seventh Street discussing diamonds and Talmud quotations with equal zeal, all Raphael could think of was that his life was over.

Until the following day, when he once again entered the bookshop and saw her standing there in all her splendor. Glancing toward the exit, he mumbled something unintelligible. She took his arm and led him to a coffee shop: 'Is this all right with you?' Yes, it was all right with him. Anxiously he followed her in, not knowing what to expect. They sat down: Raphael's head was brimming with images, fantasies, confusing insights: I'm in love, how idiotic to fall in love with a stranger, especially since she is probably leading me on. He stole a glimpse at her. She still had that teasing look on her face. She handed him a book of poetry: 'Here,' she said. 'This is for you, since you like to read so much.' He looked at the title but did not see it; he saw nothing. 'My name is Tiara,' she said. 'And yours?' Tiara, Tiara, funny name. Hungarian? Italian? It suited her. 'And yours?' she repeated. Raphael did not understand: Mine? My what? He had forgotten his name; now he remembered. She repeated it as if she were learning it by heart, then she continued: 'I find you attractive, young but attractive. How old are you?' Raphael would have done anything not to answer. He answered anyway: 'Twenty-one, well, almost.' Tiara grimaced: 'I hope you like older women.' He would have liked to say, No, I don't. And also, Yes, I do. And also, Who cares? I love you. Of course, he said none of these things; he simply answered, 'Oh, you know . . .'

That was how it began. What followed was nobody's fault. Tiara had warned him that she was older than he. Why did she leave him? She left him because she was afraid. 'I'm afraid,' she said, 'that my love will outlast yours.'

A damp, oppressive heat lingered over the Rovidok ghetto. White sky, ominous clouds. The humble houses resembled weary faces and the faces resembled broken stones marked by misery, sculpted in the expectation of death. In the streets and alleys, people breathed and spoke haltingly, ever more haltingly. It is going to pour, Hayim told himself.

He passed old acquaintances; nobody greeted him, nobody recognized him. He felt like a ghost, a dead man walking toward his grave.

He was, in fact, unrecognizable, this young man who had set out for the Holy Land just a few months ago. Faltering under the weight of his memories, he moved like an old man, like a man condemned. His eyes stared ahead like those of someone for whom past and present were blurred. With his rags, his wild beard, he looked like a wandering beggar.

'Aharon Lipkin, the schoolteacher, does he still live on this street?' he asked a real beggar, who was holding out his hand.

As he spoke his father's name, a cramp gripped his stomach: What if his father and mother were no longer alive? What if . . .?

'Aharon Lipkin,' he repeated. 'The teacher?'

The beggar did not answer. The cramp became more violent, an iron glove squeezing his insides. The beggar still did not answer. Hayim was about to turn away when he heard a sound not unlike a death rattle, 'Yes, there . . .' The beggar pointed. 'A few houses . . .'

'Thank you. And forgive me. I wish I had something for you.'

They're alive, he thought. They're here, just a few steps away . . . Thank you, God.

He tried to run; he could not. And so he dragged himself to the next corner, where he heard faint sounds coming from a cellar. At the cellar door he stopped. His father, a heavy book resting on his lap, huddled in a corner surrounded by pupils. In the uncertain light struggling through the small window, they looked unreal. Hayim opened the door wide. Aharon raised his head and held back a cry. The children turned to see who had entered.

'Hayim,' said Aharon. 'Stay where you are. I want to see you in the light.'

The light? Hayim wondered. What light?

'Hayim,' said Aharon, 'you came back. You look so tired, so thin. And all this time I thought you were safe in the land of Israel.'

'Father,' answered Hayim quietly, 'there is no more land of Israel.'

'Hush, don't say that,' said Aharon, moving closer. 'One must never say such a thing.'

He touched his son's face with such tenderness that Hayim felt close to tears.

'You'll tell us everything later,' said Aharon.

'Where is Mother? Is she all right?'

'Thank God, yes. Your sisters too.'

'Raphael?'

'He'll be here in one hour.'

Aharon returned to his pupils. Hayim found himself a place near the door.

'Next week is Tisha b'Av,' said Aharon. 'The ninth day of the month of Av. We are in the midst of preparations.'

Hayim felt like telling him that the day commemorating the destruction of the Temple and the end of Jewish sovereignty should be abolished since it was no longer the saddest day of the year. But his filial respect was too great. Instead of speaking up, he rested his head on his hands and listened.

Aharon read from the Talmud, the hallucinatory pages describing the last hours of Jerusalem: the last battle. The victory of the Romans. The arrival of Titus at the sanctuary, where he provoked the God of Israel with his obscenities. The flames rising to the sky if not higher. And the young priests ascending to the Temple roof to tell God: 'Here are the keys to your dwelling.' And a fiery hand reaching down from heaven to take them back.

We have seen worse, thought Hayim. We have seen worse than the defeat of an army. Worse than the destruction of Jerusalem.

Stanislav was worse. Kolomey was worse. Kamenetz-Podolsk was worse. At least there was a record of the fall of Jerusalem. Who would be left to record the death of an entire people? For that was what was happening; he was convinced of it.

His thoughts went back to Rika, to the Jewish community of Szerencsefalu, and he felt like interrupting his father's reading and telling him, 'Father, please! Let's forget about the past. Let's worry about the present. We are all in danger. The entire Jewish people is in danger, mortal danger!' But he held his tongue. I came back to speak my mind, he thought. I came back and I have said nothing. At that moment, sensing a presence behind him, he turned his head.

'Hayim,' sobbed Raphael. 'You're back, you're back from Jerusalem!'

'Yes, I'm back, little brother. But not from Jerusalem . . .'

Together they went outside.

'I've missed you so much,' said Raphael. 'I don't want to be away from you ever again.'

Out in the street, Hayim stared at the emaciated passersby, at the decaying houses that reeked of putrefaction.

'It's not so bad,' said Raphael, guessing his brother's thoughts. 'We get by. Mother works in the infirmary. Ruth and Hannah work for the health services. Esther is keeping house for the president of the *Judenrat*.'

'Any news from Ezra? From Yoel?'

'None. But that doesn't mean anything, does it?'

'You're right,' lied Hayim. 'It doesn't mean anything.'

'Of course, when the Germans appear, we panic. They never leave without killing at least a dozen Jews.'

'Is there no place to hide?'

'People do hide in attics, in cellars. But it doesn't help. They shoot through the doors and windows. Then they kill the first ones to come out, or the last. With them, you never know.'

Hayim almost said, 'Yes, we do know. They have decided to annihilate our people.' But he kept quiet.

The ghetto seemed more crowded than ever. That was because the Jews from the neighboring villages had been crammed into it: The *Judenrat* was ordered to lodge and feed them. At first, the Jews of Rovidok made no effort to conceal their resentment. They treated the newcomers as intruders. Fortunately, after a few weeks, the tension subsided.

'Among the new arrivals,' said Raphael, 'was our Uncle Beinish.'

'With his family?'

'No, alone. Aunt Have died of pneumonia. Our cousins Yankel and Isi were arrested and sent to the Lublin ghetto.'

'I'd like to see Uncle Beinish again.'

'Fine,' said Raphael. 'We'll stop and see him, it's on our way home.' They found Beinish in front of the barracks. The welfare service was distributing food coupons, and a lethargic line stretched to the end of the street. Hayim went up to his uncle, shook his hand, and asked how he felt.

'I have no strength left,' said Beinish. 'My legs won't carry me anymore.'

'I'll take your place,' volunteered Raphael.

Beinish would have accepted gladly, but the people in line protested.

'It's all right, I'll manage,' he said.

Suddenly, he remembered something:

'Say, Hayim, aren't you supposed to be in Palestine?'

'That's a long story, Uncle. Let's not talk about it now.'

'I see, I see.'

The two brothers took leave of their uncle and went home.

'It hurts,' said Raphael.

'What hurts?'

'To see Uncle Beinish like that. Broken. Defeated. Do you remember the presents he used to send us? I loved to visit him in his village. His garden . . . do you remember his garden?'

'I remember.'

'His horses, do you remember them?'

'I remember.'

'And his huge Shabbat candelabrum? His silver snuffbox?'

'I remember.'

'Sometimes I think it would be better to forget.'

Hayim did not answer.

'Don't you think I'm right?'

'Perhaps, little brother. Only there are things one cannot forget. Besides, I wouldn't want to.'

Raphael looked at him intently. 'I so wanted to hear about life in Jerusalem.'

'I can only tell of the death of Jerusalem.'

'Don't say that, Hayim. You mustn't talk like that.'

They walked the rest of the way in silence. The sun was setting, leaving the ghetto under a film of red dust. Their mother was standing in the doorway. She embraced Hayim and wept.

That evening, in the presence of the whole family, Hayim described his stay in Szerencsefalu, the generosity of its Jews, the peaceful conditions that prevailed there, the capricious policies of the Hungarian government.

'Then why did you come back?' asked his mother.

'There were complications. Anyway, I chose to come home and be with you.'

'You speak of complications,' said Aharon. 'What were they?'

'Oh, it's hard to explain. A guide was arrested. A network was uncovered. A ship's captain in Romania changed his mind. That sort of thing.'

'Yes, I see,' said Aharon, rubbing his temples.

They talked until late into the night. When the others had gone to bed, Hayim asked his father to go out into the courtyard with him.

'I lied to you, Father. I want you to know the truth. The truth is that the Germans will kill us, all of us. I know it for a fact. Do you want to know where I got my information?'

'I do.'

And so Hayim told him of the fate of the Jewish deportees of Szerencsefalu. How when they arrived in Galicia, they were taken to a forest near Kolomey where they were ordered to dig vast pits. Then they were shot. Every one of them. By a miracle, he, Hayim, had fallen into the pit before the bullet struck him.

'I saw everything,' he said. 'The old men whispering the *Shma Israel*. The rabbis reciting the *Vidui*. The mothers stroking the heads of their dead children. The children who, to the last second, tried not to cry. Father, I saw everything, I heard everything as I lay there among the corpses. The corpses protected me, Father. I waited until nightfall to climb out of the pit. I ran away from the dead, from their staring eyes, their tangled bodies. I ran like a wild animal until I found a stream where I washed the blood from my face, my hands, my clothes. I was covered with blood. I looked like a slaughterer. I moved only at night. I saw the mass graves, the ones in Stanislav and in Kamenetz-Podolsk. I understood that the same fate was awaiting all Jews, make no mistake. I had to tell you this, Father. Now that you know, what will you do? What will we do?'

Aharon leaned against a wall, his eyes searching the sky. Was he interrogating it? Was he begging it to open itself to the prayers of the People of the Prayer? He stood quietly for a long time, then he motioned his son to come closer:

'There is so much in all this I don't understand,' he said, his eyes still fixed on the sky. 'I believed, I was taught to believe, that man is good, that he is superior not only to animals but also to the angels. What is our religion if not an exaltation of man, the basis for God's glory? Could I have been wrong? The killers of Kolomey are men. The killers here are men. Yes, my son, there is much I do not understand.'

Hayim had never felt so close to his father. He wanted to take his hand and kiss it to mark their reunion. His shyness held him back.

'Father,' he said. 'what must I do?'

'You must tell the facts, but . . .'

'But?'

'. . . nobody will believe you. They'll accuse you of spreading panic.'

'Are you telling me to keep silent?'

'My son, having survived, it is your duty to testify. Even if people won't believe you, you have an obligation to speak. But not to just anyone. I'll call together a few men I trust. You will repeat to them what you have just told me . . .'

Aharon seemed lost in thought and Hayim dared not disturb him. Finally, Aharon spoke:

'A long time ago, I made you read the medieval martyrologies, do you remember? There was a story that also took place around the time of Tisha b'Av. A man – was it Mordekai Yossef Hakohen of Avignon? – said, "I am ashamed to relate all that the Cossacks did to us, I am ashamed to speak of it for it would be a blasphemy of man whom God created in His image." As for you, Hayim, don't be ashamed. Speak. Tell what happened. A victim must never be ashamed.'

On the eve of Tisha b'Av, Aharon invited a group of prominent men of the ghetto to his home. He chose a day when Jews were known to gather, so as not to attract the attention of informers. And because that date was symbolic.

After the customary recitation of litanies, he closed his prayer book and asked his guests to stay.

'Tonight we are in mourning; we mourn the destruction of the Temple in Jerusalem. I mourn much more. I mourn the death of our brothers and sisters assassinated by a merciless enemy thirsting for Jewish blood. Listen, I beg of you. Listen to what my son Hayim has to tell you. The message he bears has been entrusted to him by the dead.'

In simple, unemotional words, Hayim described his memories of Kolomey. As he spoke, he could see, in the yellow candlelight, the disbelief on their pale, sickly faces.

And he could see the terror in Raphael's eyes. A stunned silence followed his account. Dr Breitman, the physician, shook his head over and over. Rabbi Perl studied his fingers. The former president of the community, the timber merchant Jakobson, looked perturbed. Without a word, he got up and left. The others followed him out of the room.

Aharon and his son looked at one another.

'You did your duty,' Aharon said. 'If they refuse to listen, that's their mistake. As for us, we shall do what we must.'

That night, Aharon decided to move his family out of the ghetto and into hiding with a Christian family. He himself did not know any, but his brother Beinish did. With a little money and a few small pieces of family jewelry, Hayim succeeded in buying the complicity of a Jewish policeman, and the silence of a Polish one. There remained the task of finding a hideout. Beinish was consulted, and he suggested they go to the home of a former associate, Janek, a decent and devout man who lived alone with his wife, Jadwiga, some ten kilometers from Rovidok. A departure date was set. They would leave immediately after the High Holy Days. Hayim would have preferred not to delay, but his father refused to leave his community before Rosh Hashanah and Yom Kippur. They did not regret their decision, for, just before the holidays, they had the joy of welcoming back Ezra, who had returned from the Lodz ghetto alone, without his birds.

'Don't touch me,' says Nadav. 'One must never touch the dead. Do you understand what I'm saying? Stay right where you are. A little distance, please, a little respect for the dead. We are dangerous, has no one ever told you that? If not, it's time you learned. One must not come too close to the dead. Above all, one must never ever touch them.'

He is called Nadav, like the son of Aharon the High Priest. Young and handsome, with nostrils flaring, hands clasping and unclasping, he acts like an animal ready to pounce. He threatens in a tone that brooks no appeal. One wrong word and Raphael will be struck down.

Despite his fiery temperament, his diction is careful, his voice melodious. He has time, plenty of time. No one is waiting for him. Of course, he does speak, listen, eat, and dream. He sees no reason why the dead cannot also do these things.

He takes himself for Nadav because Nadav died by fire. When he reminisces, his gaze becomes distant, dreamy.

'You see me, right? You see my body, right? You are mistaken, my poor friend. I am nothing but a handful of ashes. My face is made of ashes. My chest is filled with ashes. And yet, the fire has never gone out. I feel it devouring me. I burn and burn, and the sea itself could not extinguish the flames that consume me.'

His eyes both seek and avoid Raphael's. Raphael would like to do something for him. He is moved by his eloquence, his fervor. But how can one help someone who dwells in the kingdom of the dead?

'My story,' says Nadav, 'does it interest you? Would you like me to tell it to you?'

'Yes, I would.'

'You're not afraid?'

'I am, but never mind. You see, I'm afraid of the dead, but I like their stories.'

Nadav calms down. He runs his right hand through his hair, letting it linger.

'I had a brother,' he says, squinting as if to remember him better. 'His name was Avihu. He too died by fire, but his story is different from mine. I can see him before me but you cannot. He is dead, but he does not live in death as I do. I screamed when I felt the first flames on my body; he did not. He looked startled. No: amazed. That's it: he was amazed. Death took him by surprise. He was prepared for anything except death. As for me, I had always been wary of death and thus had seen it approaching. In fact, that's how I succeeded in outwitting the angel of death. I flew on its blazing wings, but I am still alive.'

'How did it happen?' asks Raphael.

His curiosity is not feigned. He really would like to know how Nadav, having 'died' by fire, managed to stay alive. Funny, he thinks, I have accepted his story. I see his wounds, I hear his screams, I am present at his death as I am present at his resurrection.

'We loved our mother, Avihu and I,' says Nadav, carefully articulating each word. 'And we were very close. All that I possessed was his. The object of his wait was also mine. God spoke to us with the same voice, offered us the same visions of redemption, the same fears. For both of us, the meaning of God was the yearning for God.'

As he speaks, the young patient radiates a glow that seems otherworldly. This is how Raphael imagines a student in the school of prophets at the time of Elijah. Avidly reaching for beauty, truth, and revelation. Intense, fragile, sad, even desperate. But his sadness evokes no pity, it evokes terror.

If there were such a thing as song personified, it would be Nadav. He touches his hand to his forehead, and one hears the ethereal sound of a harp. He closes his eyes and it's as if a melody were rising to the seventh heaven, where, according to certain mystics, matter and spirit become one for the glory of the Creator. There, angels and seraphim ascend, motionless, toward the Divine Countenance. All around them, the world is transformed into a face, a thousand faces. Words turn into faces, as does light, as does fear, as does prayer.

'You didn't know my father,' says the young patient. 'You couldn't have. He was a man people couldn't help but listen to. For he loved them and they knew it. He loved everybody. Such was his nature. People could do anything, say anything; nothing interfered with his love for them. At first, people felt the same way about him. My father was popular. Even more so than his brother Moses, our political, military, and religious leader. When people were ill or hungry or wanted a divorce, it was to him they turned, not to Moses. My father listened, and by the very act of listening he appeased the wretched, healed the lepers, and reconciled those who had become estranged. Except that because he tried to understand all sides, he ultimately lost his credibility. One cannot, in a domestic quarrel, agree with both spouses. After a while people reproached my father for his kindness, which they now called weakness; and they derided his peacemaking which they now labeled "the politics of compromise." Did this cause him pain? I couldn't say. He never complained. But I remember an incident that brought home to us the immense sadness that emanated from him.

'I remember, it was night. A million stars pierced the blue sky hanging low over the white desert. The camp was asleep. Only I was awake. I had left the tent to attend to my needs when I saw a figure, tall and unreal, silhouetted against the darkness. It was my father. I took a few steps toward him; he did not hear me. I stopped. His aura of sadness was a wall between us. I could not move forward. I returned to the tent and roused my brother, Avihu, who was asleep. "Come," I said, "Father needs us." By the time we went back outside, Father had disappeared. We searched the surroundings of the camp with our eyes; in vain. He had probably gone to bed. "Let's go inside," said Avihu. "No," I said. "Not yet. Look." With my finger I pointed to the spot where my father had stood a moment before. "I don't see anything," said Avihu.

"Look, Avihu. Don't you see? Don't you see the sadness? Father is gone but his sadness is still there." Whereupon Avihu ran toward the spot and froze. "You are right," he said. "Our father's sadness is still here. I have just touched it."

'We stood there a long time.'

That's how it is with you, Pedro. You disappeared, but your aura is here; it has substance. I can touch it. I could also convey your suffering to others, to Nadav, for instance. But for that he must live, he must come back from the dead. Please, Pedro, help me bring him back.

Raphael hears a voice, not Pedro's but the voice of the old madman:

'Come, my boy, I'll teach you a prayer. Here it is: Lord, since I am suffering, I not only accept my suffering. I yearn for it, I invoke it. Lord, since suffering exists, give it to me so that I may understand those it strikes. God of my fathers, throw me into the flames so that I may emerge at peace with myself. Break me in two so that I may become whole. Push me toward darkness so that I may discover your hidden face.'

The old madman steps aside and Pedro comes to take his place. *I need your faith, Pedro. I need your strength. And yet you too seem desperate. I hear you talking to yourself: 'Man hopes, but his hope is in vain; man prays, but his prayer is futile; man weeps, but his tears are false. Nothing is achieved on this earth, admit it: our heads are weary and our conscience is heavy. Both the air and the light are noxious and stifling. You want to live? Who tells you, wanderer, that you have the right to live?'*

I am convinced that you are in danger. That you are on the verge of despair. Please don't, Pedro. Forgotten words come rushing back: To live can be a denial of life; to live can be a denial of death; to die while living is forbidden. How am I to prevent you from dying alive? Remember you said: 'It may not be in man's power to erase society's evil, but he must become its conscience; it may not be in his power to create the glories of the night, but he must wait for them and describe their beauty.'

It was to find you again that I sought out this strange place where thought and passion seem out of step, and time itself seems unhinged. Could you be mad too? Could you be trying to lure me into this bizarre adventure? No, Pedro, you are not insane. It's me, I have always been drawn to madness.

Long ago, in an essay on friendship, Raphael had written: 'Who is Pedro? A philosopher of the lower depths? A poet who has chosen exile? His voice cuts a trail of shadow through the shadows. It suggests endless meadows, darker than dark forests, immense solitudes. Some find it disquieting, others find it soothing.'

They had met in Rovidok in September of '45. Raphael had been roaming through the desolate house he had just reclaimed. He should have been making plans, but he did not feel up to it; he did not feel up to anything.

Liberated one year earlier, Rovidok had already returned to normal, thus proving that Polish towns could function very well without their Jews. With no one to speak to, nothing to do, Raphael spent his days wandering aimlessly through the streets in pursuit of ghosts. Two or three times a day he went back to his empty house and stared at the rubble: the cracked walls, the broken dishes, the shattered glass. He stayed close to 'home', just in case . . .

On that particular morning, someone opened the door without knocking. Petrified, Raphael dared not turn around and look.

'Raphael Lipkin?' called an unfamiliar voice.

Raphael was too startled to answer.

'My name is Pedro. I'm from the Briha.'

Raphael waited for the visitor to enter his field of vision. The voice belonged to a powerful man with strong features and dark green eyes.

'Is it about my parents?' Raphael asked, dreading the answer.

'No. It's about you.'

'About me?'

'I'm here to take you with me. Out of this town, out of this country.'

'But that's impossible.'

'For the Briha, *nothing* is impossible.'

That was how Raphael met Pedro and discovered the clandestine Jewish organization established to help survivors. It arranged for them to leave hostile lands and begin new lives elsewhere, especially Palestine. Part of the postwar legend, the Briha was considered omnipotent. It could provide the slip of paper that would open frontiers. Among the remnant Jewish communities, the word was that the Briha could get you out of anywhere but your grave. Some contended that it could do even that.

'How did you find me?'

'Easy. Our agents crisscross Poland and all of Eastern Europe, looking for young people like you. We find them in monasteries, convents, and the homes of Christian families. It is our job to bring them back to the Jewish people.'

Sitting on two rickety chairs in what was once the kitchen, they spoke of the past and the future like boyhood friends. The rapport between them was instantaneous. Without preliminaries, they endowed their relationship with a meaning that went beyond their understanding.

Pedro opened his satchel and took out two bottles of American lemonade. Through the window, they watched as yellow leaves floated under the autumn sky.

'When would we have to leave?'

'Today.'

'I cannot.'

'Why?'

'What about my parents, my brothers, my sisters? Imagine if they come back and don't find me here.'

'If they come back, we'll know it. We'll put them in touch with you right away, I promise.'

Deep inside, Raphael knew they would not come back. A few survivors had reappeared in Rovidok; none had brought any news of the Lipkins. It looked as if his whole family had vanished from the face of the earth. Raphael knew he was alone. And it hurt. But not as much as it would one day. That too he knew. Reluctantly, he let Pedro persuade him to leave his house, his childhood, his memories.

First stop: Lodz, where other agents of the Briha had gathered some twenty youngsters from the neighboring villages. Second stop: a displaced-persons center in Bad-Glassberg, Austria. Third stop: Paris. Wearing Russian or American uniforms, depending on the Allied zone they were in, the men of the Briha were on constant alert. They seemed familiar with every stone on every road. Their convoy was met, escorted, supplied: the quasi-military operation was carried out without incident.

The new arrivals were welcomed at a château in a suburb of Paris. The château was called Le Troupeau, 'the flock', and a hundred or more Jewish children were already there.

'Here we will rest,' Pedro told him. 'In two days, I'll show you around Paris.'

We will rest, Raphael thought. Pedro said we will rest.

Paris, 1945. City of lights? No, city of refugees. The good life for some. Not for others. Not for the suvivors, who felt out of place in the restaurants, where the food was too good; in the nightclubs, where the laughter was too loud; in the literary cafés, where the virtues of man were too easily extolled.

It was a time of easy ambitions and victories, of poetry, of black marketeering, of political commitments and philosophical experiments, of Communist slogans and Zionist demonstrations. Of châteaux commandeered for refugees in transit. Of illegal but sometimes profitable trips through Europe. For the French, it was a time of celebration: a new beginning; American officers and GIs at the Opéra and Pigalle. Long live English! Long live those who love one another, if only for an hour! Long live free love! Happiness? It can be obtained with little boldness or much money. Just don't ask too many questions. And stop mourning! Yes, the world is broken, yes, it has to be rebuilt. Never mind, cheer up: hope is not dead!

As if to make up for lost time, people plunged into wild adventures. Careers, living arrangements, even spouses were decided upon in an instant. A drink with a stranger made him a friend for life. A young woman smiled at you? One promised to love her until death do us part. A quick trip to Italy? Why not. To Tangiers? Good idea. To India? Sounds great. Every proposition was entertained, every challenge accepted. Europe was in ruins, but Europeans were ready to rejoice for any reason or no reason at all.

Le Troupeau harbored adolescents from every corner of the Continent. They spoke many languages, but mostly Yiddish. The counselors did their best to re-create for them a semblance of normality. Not easy. Some had been in the camps; others, like Raphael, had spent too much time in silence and solitude. All had grown up too quickly. They seemed older than their teachers; they knew more about life and death.

A rabbi had come to Le Troupeau to celebrate the High Holy Days. The rabbi prayed, the children listened. The rabbi recited the liturgical passages, the children listened.

'Don't you know how to read?' asked the rabbi.

No answer. He repeated the question.

Finally one of the older boys spoke up:

'We know how. But we don't want to.'

The rabbi, wrapped in his ritual shawl, closed his prayer book and said, 'Children, you are right. Perhaps we need a different kind of prayer.'

And he began to weep soundlessly, until he was choked with sobs. As Raphael looked at him more closely, his blood turned to ice. Impossible, he murmured, impossible. It was the old man, the old madman with the veiled eyes. Yes, it was he. He closed his eyes and saw himself back in Rovidok at New Year's services. 'Who shall live and who shall die? . . .' He remembered a story. The story of a young shepherd who once took part in the most sacred of Yom Kippur prayers, the prayer of *Neilah* which closes the service. The rabbi was silent, deep in meditation. It was an uneasy silence, a silence signifying that something grave was taking place in heaven. An hour went by and the rabbi was still in a trance. The faithful felt threatened and wished to help the rabbi reverse the evil fate. The shepherd too felt this need. Since he did not know how to pray, he took out his flute and began to play a nostalgic tune. The faithful were horrified and ready to chastise him. But the rabbi smiled at the shepherd: 'Thank you,' he said, 'you have saved us; an innocent tune sometimes does more good than all the prayers in the world.'

'Thank you rabbi, your tears have freed us,' said one of the older boys. 'Now we can pray.'

At the end of services, Raphael asked the rabbi, 'Do you remember me?'

The rabbi responded: 'The Day of Judgment is also a day of memory.'

Raphael lost his composure. 'I am from Rovidok.'

'Rovidok, Rovidok,' said the rabbi, nodding. 'A beautiful Jewish community. Swallowed. Not completely, since you are here. Don't let yourself be swallowed, my boy. As long as you're alive, the dead live on inside you. Don't let death swallow you, too.'

It was the old man, Raphael was certain. The old madman with the veiled eyes. He tried to look into the rabbi's eyes, but he had bowed his head.

If only Pedro were here. Pedro must have known him. It may even have been Pedro who brought him out of Rovidok. But by the time Pedro arrived, the rabbi was gone.

'No, I don't know the rabbi,' he told Raphael. 'The Briha has many agents. I'm not the only one who organizes border crossings.'

'What about Rovidok, is there any news?'

'None.'

'What if someone is there right now, looking for me?'

'We would know.'

Raphael could have joined an illegal convoy to Palestine, but he preferred to wait for the possible return of one of his brothers or sisters. To pass the time, he studied. The counselors insisted on teaching him French. After all, why not? Two hours a day, not so bad. Besides, he was not alone. There were fifteen other students in his group. A girl, the only girl in his class, reminded him of his sister Esther, even though she was not shy like Esther. When she recited a poem, she seemed to be speaking directly to him. Her name was Blanca. She was vivacious and her laughter was warm and seductive. The boys were crazy about her, even those who liked other girls. As for Raphael, he didn't look at any girl, not even at her. But he listened to her. And that was enough.

At Shabbat meals, Blanca sang the traditional melodies with

the others. Her voice was so beautiful, it tore him apart. When he finally admitted to himself that he was in love with her, he wanted to die. Fortunately, nobody noticed. Life at Le Troupeau with its counselors and social workers, and its steady stream of speakers, was too engrossing.

One evening at an outdoor get-together, he found himself sitting on the grass next to Blanca. Somebody was telling a story. Somebody else was reciting a poem. There was laughter, singing. Suddenly, Raphael realized with dismay that he had grazed Blanca's hand. Expecting to be slapped at any moment, he quickly pulled back. He could no longer hear the singing, understand the words. His whole life was concentrated in his fingers. But what was happening? Blanca's hand was clasping his. Raphael gasped. How could he breathe? Blanca moved closer; he felt her leaning against him. His head began to spin.

All that night, when sleep refused to come, he wrote love poems in Yiddish which Blanca would never read for the simple reason that she did not understand one word of that language.

But he showed them to Pedro, who found them both foolish and beautiful.

Janek and Jadwiga, honest peasants and good Christians, had built a shelter under their barn for Beinish and his brother's family. It was impossible to detect its entrance with the naked eye.

'I know it's not comfortable,' said Janek. 'But the war won't last, you'll see . . .'

Bald, with a mustache and few remaining teeth, Janek often swallowed his words. To make himself understood, he supplemented every sentence with gestures and grimaces. As for his wife, she spoke little, content to mumble words she alone could hear.

Aharon's family slept on blankets thrown over a few layers of straw. The ventilation holes had been Ezra's handiwork. Every morning, before feeding the cows in the stable next door, Janek or Jadwiga brought food: bread, vegetables, sometimes hot soup. The major worry of the clandestine tenants was noise. And so they waited for nightfall even to stretch their legs. You never knew when a neighbor might come around.

'I have faith,' said Aharon. 'God is watching over us. Otherwise, we would never have gotten out of the ghetto.'

In truth, it had been easy. All it took was money. There was no shortage of corrupt policemen, inside or outside the ghetto. And the nights were black. And the German soldiers tired. Between midnight and 4 A.M., the family had crossed to the other side in pairs. Forty-eight hours later, they all met at Janek and Jadwiga's. When they entered the shelter, they were confident that they would last out the war.

Their disappearance drew few comments in the ghetto. People were always being taken away, imprisoned or deported by the Germans. When the schoolboys came home with the news that *heder* was closed, or rather, that the schoolteacher and his family were no longer there, everyone's reaction had been: those poor Lipkins, somebody must have turned them in. Aharon should have been more careful; didn't he know that schools were forbidden in the ghetto?

Aharon went on studying and teaching in his subterranean quarters. He had taken along as many books as he could carry, and he insisted that the whole family devote several hours a day to reading, prayer, and meditation – even Rivka, who had to look after everyone's food and clothing. At night, they went out in pairs to wash. As for their bodily functions, Ezra had taken care of the problem by placing an old wine barrel in a corner shielded by a thick wall. Under the circumstances, they were well provided for.

'God willing, we'll survive,' said Aharon.

'God willing, God willing,' mumbled Beinish. 'Let Him be willing to put an end to this war!'

'Beinish!' his brother scolded him. 'Don't blaspheme! Not here, not now!'

'Can you think of a better place, a more propitious moment, to blaspheme?'

The murmured exchange soon degenerated into an argument. The constant enforced closeness, the lack of privacy, tried everyone's nerves.

Beinish was the first to rebel. Too old, too independent, he couldn't tolerate his brother's authority. He objected to study and prayer.

'I don't have patience for this,' he said. 'Zion is far away and so is God. I have other concerns. More urgent ones.'

'Don't blaspheme, Beinish, not here!' Aharon warned.

'Listen, Aharon, nobody tells me how to behave! I'm not one of your *heder* pupils!'

Rivka begged them to stop, in vain. The argument went on, more violent than ever. It was Ezra who finally prevailed. 'Shshsh!' he said. 'I hear something. There must be a stranger at the farm.' An ingenious device, which he used more than once. If it wasn't Aharon and Beinish, it was the brothers and sisters bickering over ancient grievances: 'You said this, you did that, the day when . . .'

'I've had it,' Beinish declared in the fourth month of their forced cohabitation. 'There are too many of us. I foresee a disaster. I'm leaving.'

'Where will you go?' asked Aharon.

'Don't worry about me. I know my way around this region.'

With Jadwiga's help, he sought out a woodsman who agreed to shelter him for a while.

'I don't trust that man,' said Janek. 'Beinish was foolish to go off alone.'

Still, his departure did alleviate some of the tension. A period of respite followed. Until the day Esther began to cough. First she complained of a terrible pain in her throat. Then it was her head, her chest. Then her temperature began to rise. She became delirious. She needed a doctor urgently. Janek and Jadwiga knew of none in the village. Wringing her hands, Jadwiga said, 'When we are sick, we go all the way to Rovidok.'

'Yes, we go all the way to Rovidok,' repeated Janek, pointing in that direction. 'Our doctor lives in the ghetto. He is a Jew.'

And so, Ezra returned to the ghetto, found a doctor, described his sister's symptoms, and came back with medication.

'God is good,' said Aharon. 'He watches over you. I bless you, my son. May you continue to outwit the enemy.'

'The road from Lodz to Rovidok was far more dangerous, Father. What's more, the German who will catch me has not been born!'

And yet, Esther died and Ezra was caught.

Aharon resigned himself to burying his daughter in the farmyard, making Janek and Jadwiga promise they would point out the site to the Jewish community if the worst came about and none of the family survived the war. Ezra had another idea: he wanted to carry his sister to the Jewish cemetery. She deserved to rest in consecrated ground.

'It's too dangerous, my son,' warned his father. 'Jewish law forbids us to expose ourselves to such dangers.'

'You're thinking of the law and I'm thinking of my sister,' retorted Ezra, immediately regretting his words.

'Forgive me, Father. But you see, I feel guilty. What if I brought back the wrong medicine? Esther may have died because of me.'

Aharon wanted to reassure his son, but before he could, Rivka had kissed Ezra on the forehead. Then Ezra, his eyes filled with tears, locked himself into a silence that lasted the entire week of *shivah*.

The days, resembling one another, turned into weeks, the weeks became months. Until, finally, winter released its grip and the forest opened itself to the sun; the ground rejected the ice and snow. The sound of a rushing stream reached the shelter just as Purim was approaching. It would not be easy for Aharon to celebrate the holiday. Since Esther's death, he had been unable to conceal his despair.

One morning, Janek arrived with frightening news. Informers were stalking the countryside like wolves on the prowl.

'You should split up,' he said. 'I'm telling you this for your own sake. That way, there may still be a chance for some of you.'

'Where could we go?' asked Aharon.

'I have a cousin in the village of Kozlava. And an uncle not far from Faristov. And another uncle in Tomaszov. I trust them. Of course, if you were able to pay, it would be better . . .'

'I have no more money, Janek.'

'It would be better if you did. But never mind. We'll have to do without it.'

Aharon and Rivka decided to take Janek's advice. It made sense to separate.

'Before going into battle, Jacob did the same thing,' said

Aharon. 'He divided his family into two camps. If one perished, the other still had a chance.'

Ruth and Hannah would go to Janek's cousin, Hayim to Janek's uncle in Faristov, Rivka and Aharon to his uncle in Tomaszov. Ezra and Raphael would stay at the hideout.

Their parting was brief: a few words, a few gestures.

'God willing,' said Rivka, 'we shall meet again at home.'

'God willing,' repeated Aharon.

In the darkness, he whispered to his sons, 'Don't forget to observe Shabbat. Or the High Holy Days. Don't forget to put on your *tephillin*. Don't forget that you are Jews.'

The hideout now seemed huge and empty. Raphael nestled against his brother. There were questions he wanted to ask, but he dared not: Would he ever see his parents again? His sisters? Hayim? Yoel? Would the war ever end? How long could he and Ezra hold out underground?

To ease his little brother's anguish, Ezra stroked his hair. 'Everything will be all right, Raphael. You'll see. We'll stay together. To the end. You'll see.'

'Yes, Ezra,' said Raphael without conviction.

'I'll take care of you. You know me. I can handle anything. Those swine will never hurt us again.'

For Raphael, Ezra was now his whole family, his whole world. Ezra took care of him, gently urging him to eat, to say his prayers, and to write letters he would one day give to their parents. To pass the time, Ezra told Raphael stories he had brought back from Lodz. Bird stories. The kind, he said, that birds tell one another upon returning from their migrations, or at night before falling asleep. Raphael listened enthralled.

'Birds have their own god. Did you know that?' Ezra asked.

No, Raphael had no idea.

'Like ours, their god too lives up above. And every morning

the birds recite their prayers to him. Listen to the one I like best. "Lord," they say, "let us be seen by a good person."'

As long as Ezra was at his side, Raphael did not fear the enemy. He feared only one thing: that Ezra would leave him.

Which was what happened.

As the High Holy Days approached, Ezra became restless.

'What do you think? Shall I go visit our parents?' he asked. 'Your letters will be their New Year's presents.'

'I'll come with you.'

'Impossible.'

'But I want to see them, too.'

'We'll both be caught.'

'But I want to see them, too.'

'No,' Ezra decreed. 'We can't risk it.'

'You promised you would never leave me.'

'I'm not leaving you. I'll only be gone a few hours. Alone I'll be safe. I have a good nose; I can smell a German ten kilometers away.'

Ezra left at dawn, and Raphael quickly fell into a panic. Fighting to stay calm, he kept getting up to see if his brother was back. Ezra, Ezra, where are you? You've been gone so long. What about your promise?

He made so much noise that Janek came to warn him:

'Are you trying to alert the police?'

'Ezra hasn't come back.'

'Well, he shouldn't have left.'

'He's gone. He won't come back.'

'Of course he will, you'll see. Ezra is clever. He'd find his way back from hell itself.'

He didn't.

When Ezra had not returned by nightfall, Janek went

looking for him and brought back the news: Ezra had been caught near the cemetery. Had he seen his parents? Janek did not know.

Crazed with grief, Raphael threw himself on the mud floor. He stopped eating, drinking, praying; all he did was sleep. That was how he spent the New Year and Yom Kippur. For the first time, he did not mark them with confession and penance. Jadwiga did her best to console him. She tried to make him drink tea and vodka, she even brought him hot water for washing. But there was no consoling him. He did not even yearn for death, for he did not feel alive.

The day Janek came to give him the news that his parents, his sisters, and Hayim had all been rounded up and sent to prison, he did want to die.

'I want to join them,' said Raphael.

'Are you mad? Stay where you are. You are safe here.'

'I don't want to be safe. I want to be with my parents.'

The discussion went on until, at wits' end, Janek bolted the hideout from the outside. 'If you carry on like this, it's me they will arrest.'

Three days later, Janek brought more news:

'They're out of prison; they've been sent back to the ghetto.'

'Then I'll sneak back into the ghetto. Maybe Ezra is with them.'

At last, Janek gave in. That very evening, Raphael set out for Rovidok, which he reached after hours of walking, running, and hiding. He didn't rest until he saw the ghetto, a mass of darkness encircled with barbed wire. He lifted a section of wire fence and slipped inside unseen by the policemen patrolling the entrance. Keeping close to the ground, he came to the narrow street leading to the infirmary. As he stood up, he heard a whisper: 'Here. Come over here.'

The voice from the shadows asked him who he was.

'Raphael. Raphael Lipkin. The son of Aharon the schoolteacher.'

'Oh, yes,' said the voice.

'Do you know where my father is? And the rest of my family? They're here, aren't they?'

'No, they are not.'

'I don't believe you. I was told they were all sent back to the ghetto.'

'They are gone,' said the voice. 'The Germans are liquidating the ghetto. Your family left with the first transport.'

So this will never end, Raphael thought. The blows keep coming.

'The second transport leaves tomorrow,' said the voice.

'I'll be there.'

'Don't.'

'Why not?'

'It is written somewhere,' said the voice firmly, 'that you shall stay behind. Always. You are meant to see and never forget. I'll lead you to a place from which you'll be able to see all, record all. Just promise me you'll stay quiet. Promise me you'll survive. To await the return of those who have gone. To welcome them into your memory. You will become their final resting place.'

Though exhausted, Raphael argued: He wanted to go to his parents. Wherever they were, they were probably waiting for him. He refused to live without them.

'To refuse to live,' said the voice, 'is an act of treason not only toward the living, but also toward the dead. I speak to you in the name of both. To die now would be cowardice. Make the more difficult choice: to live without the dead, to live and remember the dead.'

'I don't believe you. They are not dead!'

'You're right, my boy. They are alive. In me and in you.

These men and women, these sages and madmen who have carried the Word – and have been carried by it. Observe them, allow them to take root inside you. They have lived as you live, as I have lived and died, under a blue sky, with memories made of whispers and silences, and a yearning for innocence. Do you understand what I am saying?'

The longer he listened to the voice, the more familiar it sounded to Raphael. It reverberated inside him; it spiraled up into the sky and wound itself around the stars. It brought him back to his childhood with its peaceful Shabbat, its exultant songs and dreams. It brought him back to the beginning of his people's adventure that was now ending in madness and doom.

Raphael leaned over: yes, it was the old madman with the veiled eyes.

'Don't you recognize me?' asks the patient. 'I was your friend, I still am. I often think of our escapades, of the close calls we survived, of the mischief we got ourselves into as if we were the Lord's peers. What, you don't remember? How could you forget?'

Though Raphael knows the patient is mad, he listens attentively. Since his arrival at the clinic, he has come to mistrust his first impressions. Maybe the patient is telling the truth. Maybe they once knew each other. During the war? In Paris? But he has no recollection.

'One of us must have changed,' says the patient, examining his fingernails after polishing them with a filthy handkerchief. 'Yes, one of us. It must be me. Death has a way of changing us, you know.'

Here we go again, Raphael tells himself; it's an obsession with these patients. If this keeps up, Benedictus will have to build a funeral parlor. To make himself feel better, he turns his thoughts to someone who was, and remains, a symbol of life for him.

A series of images: Pedro, the convoy leader in Rovidok. Pedro, the fearless rescuer of orphans in France. Pedro, the spellbinding storyteller. Pedro, on a train headed for Madrid. Pedro, poring over a notebook, writing slowly, carefully. What was he writing? A paean to savage gods? A litany to the memory of their victims? Calm, at peace with himself, he not only writes in silence, he writes silence itself.

'Pedro, where are you?' You lift your head and a thousand shadows flee: 'I'm here, Raphael, I'm here.'

'I've never seen you so alone.' After a long pause, you answer patiently, 'Death changes us, you know.' I am incredulous. 'You, dead? For me you are immortal.'

'I am not speaking of myself. I am speaking of the others. Their death changes us.'

Raphael is distracted from his thoughts by the patient, who is snorting and stamping his feet. 'You ignoramus! You don't know who I am? Do you know who *you* are? Tell me, who are you? What is your name? Your father's name? What are you waiting for? Answer me. Hurry up, the angel will come any minute.'

The patient is getting increasingly agitated. He seems to be trapped in his own game. Right now, he is the angel inquisitor, interrogating, manipulating. He is the master and it is up to Raphael to obey, to justify himself. Raphael waits for him to run out of breath, which only enrages the patient further.

'So, you don't deign to respond. For you the past doesn't seem to matter, nothing matters. You think you owe me nothing, not even the courtesy of an introduction, just because I'm dead?'

Abruptly, the patient calms down. Raphael wonders: Does he even see me? And who am I to him? 'I'll be happy to introduce myself,' he says.

'Go ahead,' says the patient. 'Pretend you don't know me. But I know you. The dead have better memories than the living. Me, I remember everything. Our first handshake. The first time you drank to my health. Our first disagreement. Do you remember any of it?'

Raphael shakes his head.

The patient looks skeptical. 'You can't fool me. Admit it, you remember me, but you don't believe I'm dead.'

Raphael does not know what to say.

'It's terrible,' whines the patient.

'What's terrible?'

'If I'm not dead, I'll have to die all over again.'

He buries his face in his hands. Is he crying? Anyway, he quickly pulls himself together.

'Very well. You leave me no choice. I am going to tell you about my death:

'I was ill, you do remember that, don't you? My body had turned against me. The enemy was churning inside, punishing me. It's the heart, said the first doctor. The lungs, said the second. No, the kidneys, said the third, without a moment's hesitation. Each one had his own diagnosis, and all the while I suffered. Each one examined me, prodded me, pricked me, and all the while I suffered. Then came two visitors. Slowly, more and more slowly, my gaze shifted from them to the four walls of my hospital room, to my poor hands, which had begun to shrivel before my eyes. My vision became blurred. My breathing stopped. My wife began to scream. I was dead but my ears continued to pick up the sounds inside the room, and beyond. I heard my wife's plea: "Do something, Doctor, do something!" And the doctor's solemn reply: "It's too late."

'Then came a long silence and the usual platitudes: one must be strong, bow to death, be accepting, and so on. In any case, *I* had accepted death. Laid out on my bed, I had at last come to terms with what was happening to me. Is that what dying means? I wondered. To hear everything? To understand everything? Not to want to change things, to move things around anymore? Unlike the living, who love to move everything, including the dead. I watched as they approached the bed, lifted me – I must admit with some care – and set me down on the floor. Why couldn't they leave me where I was? How was I disturbing them? I was no longer in pain, that was true. Was that any reason to haul me around like a sack of flour? Never mind, they could do as they pleased, I didn't care anymore. I no longer felt like protesting, or even complaining. You'd rather see me on the floor? Fine. Just be glad I'm not heavier than I am.

'So, there I was, on the floor. The room was getting crowded. Suddenly, everybody wanted to see me. I heard people whispering. Some discussed my age: "Poor fellow, he was so young." "Yes, but he was sick." Funny, how quickly people adjust to death; they already spoke of me in the past tense. For we no longer were, I was going to say, we no longer "lived," in the same time. Time for me was neither faster nor slower, merely different. It had not stopped for me; it had changed, that's all. And I? Had I changed? True, my body was inert, but that wasn't the point; the point was something else, but I couldn't put my finger on it. Oh well, there would be plenty of time to think about that later. For the moment, I listened.

'They telephoned my children. All five of them would be at the funeral. Even Simon, the eldest, would take the first flight out of Eugene, Oregon. I felt sorry for Simon. He had always had trouble coping. His wife tormented him and he did not have the courage to leave her. He was too kind. My son Charles was different; he refused to marry. Why love one woman when he could have ten? That was his philosophy. The next day all five of them had the same gloomy face. Too bad I couldn't see them. Never mind: I heard them.

'Incredible, how acute my hearing had become. I detected the faintest whisper. I could hear the breeze caressing the trees, each drop of rain falling, night invading the house. I could hear the raising of an eyelid, the trembling of a lip, the wringing of a hand. I could hear the words that were spoken, and those that were not. I could hear the sound the earth makes as it spins. I am like Death which sees everything, only I *hear* everything. Right now, I hear everything you're saying and yet you're not saying anything at all.'

Indeed, Raphael has not said a word. He is wondering how Pedro would behave in his place. He would probably play with his pipe, or with his pen, all the while studying the patient. He might nod his head sympathetically. 'Yes, of course, you're dead. Of course, the dead hear better than the living. Of course, the dead can be eloquent. Of course, the dead remember their death.' Pedro knows how to inspire confidence. Even the dead would trust him. Only, this patient does not trust Raphael. He cannot believe that Raphael does not remember him. When he falls silent for a moment, Raphael is quick to ask how he managed to recognize him, since the dead hear but do not see.

'No mystery about that,' says the patient. 'I recognized your voice. Your voice hasn't changed even though when you rejected me, you repudiated yourself. I know you abandoned me because I'm dead. Aren't you ashamed to abandon a dead friend? You didn't even bother to come to my funeral. That was a mistake: What a spectacle you missed! God, what a crowd! You would have been amused. I heard everything, I even heard the benches creak every time the audience stood up. I was eulogized as a great man. People are such hypocrites!

'You cannot imagine the praise that was heaped on me. You would not believe how generous and pious and intelligent they said I had been. If one were to believe my eulogy, I never hurt anybody. A protector of orphans and widows, that was me. A saint, nothing less. The verdict was unanimous. Case closed. What an exhilarating experience, to be present at one's own beatification. Never in my lifetime were my children so close. They're beautiful, the tears that are shed over you once you're dead.

'The moral of the story: It's better to be dead. The wise old King Solomon, son of David, was right when he praised the dead more than the living, and chose to visit a house in mourning instead of a tavern. Death confers a dignity, a religious aura, which might otherwise be unattained. Isn't it remarkable what death can do? It really puts to shame those who try to ignore it. You, the living, are so funny. First you deny it, then you use cosmetics on it. Anything, but not death, that's your motto. You consider it the supreme enemy; its inevitability fills you with dread. I ask you, why? After all, God created death just as He created life. What would you mortals do without death? Does it not give a meaning to your futile endeavors, your ridiculous games? Does it not equalize all beings? Life divides men, death brings them closer. Life inspires envy, jealousy, greed. Death erases them. Unjust and ungrateful, that's what you are. I can say this since I am already on the other side. The question is: Do you comprehend what you hear? Do you really hear? The living, unlike the dead, cannot see beyond life. What is worse, they cannot hear the dead.'

Raphael acquiesces. The patient is right. The dead will prevail in any contest with the living. After all, they have many advantages. Above all: they are free. No longer governed by the laws of life.

'I hear you,' says Raphael. 'I hear you perfectly. Yet I am alive.'

'Are you sure?'

The patient is snickering. He's got me there. How does one prove that one is alive? By showing one's passport? One's driver's license? Is that what life is? A bundle of papers?

Raphael notices the dead man's pallor. Today he seems more nervous than usual. This is the day when his wife and daughters usually come to see him. Raphael has noticed them on earlier visits. All three show great concern for the patient. They always ask him if there is anything he needs. He always answers that it is too late.

What triggered his illness? No one seems to know. Raphael was told that he got up one night, slipped, and hit his head on a table, losing consciousness. His wife found him sprawled on the kitchen floor the next morning. At the hospital, he said to her sorrowfully, 'You shouldn't have.' That's all he said.

'You don't look well,' says Raphael, to change the subject. 'Did you sleep all right?'

'What a bore you are. Asking a dead man whether he has slept well, really . . . And you call yourself a professor . . . And you think you're alive . . . Soon you'll ask me whether I made love last night . . . Don't worry, I slept beautifully. That's not the point. The point is . . . my dreams. The dead do dream, you know. Just like you. Better than you. Our nightmares, do you know what they are? Your reality, that's what. The reality of the living. Don't you know that, you fool?'

While Raphael waits for him to calm down, he wonders: Did Pedro know this man? Is he the witness I'm looking for? It is now almost forty days since I arrived at the clinic, and still I have discovered nothing. These madmen won't rest until I too am mad. *And you, Pedro? Who will come to your defense when I am driven beyond reason? Who will proclaim your innocence? This dead madman, perhaps?*

Very well, let's continue. Let's hear the rest of his story.

'Where were we? What happened after the funeral?' asks Raphael, expecting the patient to say, 'That was it. Nothing happened.' Wrong. He launches into an elaborate description of his sojourn in the grave, one that echoes the occult tales found in Jewish medieval works.

'The most terrifying moment,' he says, 'do you want to know when it comes? When the ceremony ends. Everybody leaves and you remain alone. A prisoner in your grave. Suddenly there is silence. Total, opaque silence. The last sound has faded away. The gravediggers have gone home; their shovels are stored. You, who not an hour ago didn't miss a thing, hear nothing. And then a new fear grips you, paralyzes you, penetrates your every cell. You try to imagine the future. You cannot. You try to remember your past. You cannot. All there is inside you is fear, a savage beast that strangles you, depriving you of your last vestige of hope.'

He speaks of his death like a traveler recalling a journey to a distant land. He speaks and Raphael listens attentively. He follows the dead man so deeply into his hallucinated memories that he forgets why he came to the clinic; he forgets he is here to vindicate Pedro. At that moment, death's presence is all-pervasive, shattering his certainties.

As he speaks, the dead man gets more and more animated. He is almost shouting.

'What was I to do? How was I to find my way back? I had to reclaim the few strands of memory, the few fragments of the person I once was. I knew – I didn't understand how – but I knew that memory was a function of time. Was I to insert myself into time, any time? Was I to find a consciousness in which time would not scatter like sand on a well-traveled road? I would have succeeded if only I could have breathed, but that was out of the question. After all, you cannot ask too much of the dead: if they started breathing like everybody else, where would it all end? Anyway, let the living breathe, let them run out of breath, as far as I'm concerned. I envy them only one thing: their memory. Nothing else. Not their happiness, not their curiosity. Only their memory . . .

'In my grave, alone with my body, I suddenly realized that I was waiting for something, or somebody. I didn't know what, I didn't know who. Yes, something was going to happen, but I didn't know what it was. All I knew was that this expectation corresponded to a lesson learned in life. With considerable effort, I managed to retrace my steps. Yes, long ago I read in a dusty old volume that three days after burial, an angel comes knocking on the grave of the deceased, asking his name. Woe unto him if he has forgotten it. That's what happened to me: I forgot. I panicked: who was I? God of my forefathers, help me: who do you wish me to be? I saw my hollow face, my watery eyes, my white lips. I knew that this image of a sick old man was my own. This man was me, I knew that, but I also knew that this knowledge was not enough. I knew that this man identified himself with me, but still I was unable to guess who I was. They say a man is the sum of his experiences: his regrets, his failures, his triumphs, his silences – in short, his memory. And here I was, poor me, without memory. I could not even remember my name. And what about the angel who was about to knock on my tomb? He would ask my name and I wouldn't know what to answer. He would repeat his question and I would be forced to remain silent. The third time I failed to respond, he would seize my soul and hurl it into infinity, far from man and God. It would become irretrievable, damned for all eternity.

'It was my father who saved me. His face appeared before me. He was sad, my father. Sad to see me like this, defeated, repudiated. I knew that he was dead for I remembered his funeral. But I felt his presence. I was sure that *he* had not forgotten *his* name. His name, his name: if only I could remember it, I would be saved. Father, what was your name? He stared at me without answering. He looked pained. Yet the day he died he seemed peaceful, forgiving. Wrapped in his *tallit*, he seemed lost in meditation. His *tallit:* I examined his *tallit*. He used to wear it at services, at the House of Study. On Shabbat he was often invited to take part in the weekly reading of the Torah. After being called by his name and his father's, he would ascend the *bima*. Ya'amod reb Yitzhak ben Moshe: let Yitzhak son of Moshe rise and come forward. And me, how did they invite me to participate in that same ceremony? Of course: Moshe son of Yitzhak. Yes, that was it: I was given my grandfather's name. At once I felt better, reassured. Let the angel come now. I was no longer afraid. Let's say, I was less afraid. I wanted to thank my father, but he had disappeared. No doubt he had returned to his place up above, in the so-called world of truth. And once again I was alone. And alone I would be when I confronted the angel.

'Suddenly my head cleared and I knew that I owed that too to my father. I remembered the knowing light in his eyes. I recalled many things: my boyish pranks, my nightmares, my abrupt awakenings, my absurd sorrows and even more absurd ambitions, my friends, some loyal, others not so loyal. I remembered them with nostalgia. But it no longer hurt; I relived all events as though they were welded together. All places were one single place; all sensations, one single sensation. Come to think of it, I no longer had a past. Or a present. Come to think of it, time no longer flowed. That is the real victory of death: it stops time. The decades, the centuries, pile up inside the grave. Through it all, the wait goes on. I was waiting for the angel.

'Never had I waited so for anyone. I was afraid to fall back into oblivion. I knew that he was to appear three days and three nights after the burial. Having lost all sense of time, I no longer understood the meaning of those words. Three days? Three nights? How long could that be? I wanted to ask my father, but he was not coming back. Yitzhak ben Moshe, listen: Moshe ben Yitzhak, your eldest son, is calling you. But I did not speak. Not one word. I would not speak until the angel appeared.

'At last: three taps. He had arrived. He was knocking on my grave, and his three taps reverberated inside me. Raw fear. Not to forget, not to forget my name nor that of my father, not to forget who I was. But the knocking was so loud it drowned out my thoughts. Was this what our sages called the "pangs of death"? If ever I meet them up above, I will ask them. But for the moment, I was the one who was going to be questioned. The angel was about to ask the first, the most important, question: "Mortal, what is your name?" From a barely audible whisper, the voice swelled and filled my grave and my being. Would this unbearable pain never stop? Inside me a cry, a scream, was forming: Moshe son of Yitzhak! Do you hear me, angel? Stop the interrogation! Stop torturing me! You wanted my name? Here it is: Moshe son of Yitzhak. Only, the words refused to be uttered; they remained knotted inside me.

'The angel standing on my grave was silent. He was waiting for my answer, which was late in coming. And yet I knew it. I repeated it to myself, I tried to propel it out of my chest, but, woe unto me, it remained glued to my throat, to my lazy tongue, which refused to respond. I sensed the angel's impatience: "Mortal", he repeated, "what is your name?" Once more, his voice tore through me. I felt it severing every one of my arteries, sawing through every one of my nerves. What would become of me, Moshe son of Yitzhak? In addition to the pain, there was now anger and indignation. Where was justice? The angel asked me a question, I knew the answer, and yet something prevented me from answering. Who was responsible?

'And suppose I had spoken. What if the angel were deaf? That would have been some joke. The thought occurred to me because I'd heard it said that the Angel of Death was nothing but eyes: eyes from head to toe, a lethal gaze. My angel, on my very own grave, may well have been lacking ears. I protested, I insisted on reparations, I demanded justice. The angel, however, remained unmoved. He thrust his question into my grave for the third time, his voice echoing throughout the universe.

'I sensed that everywhere in the unfathomable kingdom of death, judges and witnesses, victims and spectators, all held their breath and waited to hear whether I passed the test. But, for God's sake, how could I pass the test when I was prevented from being heard? Please, God, unseal my lips! Was the angel disappointed? Not as much as I was. I had only one wish: to appear before the Celestial Tribunal and state my case, tell them that injustice exists not only in the world of falsehood and illusion, but also in the world of eternity. Tell them . . . Without a word, the angel ordered me to stop behaving like a fool. Without a move, he opened the grave. Without touching me, he cradled me in the palm of his hand, his icy and fiery hand. And the next moment, I found myself in the *Kaf Hakela*, the space outside space, outside time, far from God, far from everything. And, just as you see me today, that is where I have remained.'

When one is ill or mad, all that was before recedes. Before: my life, my work, my passions. One wants to look back as far as possible: to the brink. And beyond. Until one is back at the beginning, until one transcends that beginning.

What was the world before it emerged from chaos? What was the Word before God used it to create the universe? Where was man before Adam?

Where does thought come from? asked the great Maggid of Mezeritch. Where did it hide before entering my head?

Where was I before I was?

Before, I was a bird, Ezra would say. Before, I was the chirping of a bird, my father would say. Before, I was the branch that supported the bird. I was the rustling of the wind in the leaves. I was the soul that intercepted the rustling and offered it, like a prayer, to the lost wanderer. Before? I was a prayer.

When one is ill or mad, one simply passes through walls, no need to climb them. One reinvents all rules. On a whim, one imposes limits on oneself, knowing that a moment later, one may push them farther, too far. When one is mad, nothing is too far.

When one is mad, one wishes the whole world were mad. But when the whole world goes mad, one is unhappy. How unfair: to be both unhappy and mad.

After weeks of trying, Raphael has managed a date with Karen. They are having coffee in the library, at an hour when it is usually empty. Outside, under an amber sun, the valley seems to float toward the horizon.

The clinic is calm, bathed in stillness. An artificial stillness that is good for the patients, thank you. They are resting, thank you. Peace to all men deprived of peace.

'I don't understand you, Karen,' says Raphael for openers.

'Oh?' she says, raising her eyebrows.

The coffee is lukewarm. Raphael stirs his nervously, conscious of the cold gaze resting on his hand.

What foolishness! He is flirting with a young woman who

is not even his type, he is flirting with her and all he can think of saying is 'I don't understand you.' Does that mean he doesn't understand her behavior? But it is his own behavior that is perplexing. What madness to turn oneself into a sleuth to defend the honor of a slandered friend.

'Why are you here, Karen?' Raphael says, to say something.

'You know why. I work here.'

Is it that simple? A voice inside Raphael, a suspicious voice, one he does not like, whispers: don't be so gullible, watch out, this woman is hiding something, she is not to be trusted, she belongs to the enemy camp . . .

'Karen . . . who are you?'

'Who am *I*? *You* want to know who *I* am?'

Again, that belligerent tone. She might as well be telling him to mind his own business. Raphael wonders, is she having an affair with Benedictus? Now there's a strange one, the director. Arrogant, pedantic, he likes to play the big brother to Raphael, who finds that offensive: the director is not his brother. What is he to Karen?

'Karen, tell me, where are you from? What did you do before you came to the clinic?'

She stares at him suspiciously. 'For someone who's not a psychiatrist, you're awfully nosy.'

What is it that troubles him about Karen? Inexplicably, Tiara looms in his mind. A series of images, out of sequence, cling to one another, invade his memory: Tiara in a playful mood, Tiara in a rage. If only he could love her as he loved her long ago. If only he could love. *How does one learn to love again, Pedro? You once said: 'Mankind will founder because it has lost the capacity to worship.'* What a mess, he thinks. Since his separation from Tiara, he has known other women. Quite a few, in fact. A sensual redhead; they made love until they couldn't stand one another. A striking brunette who cried in the dark.

A Japanese violinist with a passion for Bach. They are all one. He has always been like that: he sees in every new woman *the* woman of his life. And for one night, one week, that is what she is. Was Karen next?

She looked startled. Why? He has not said a word. Could she be reading his thoughts? If so, she would also guess the reason for his sojourn among the insane. The only remedy: he must think of something else, anything else. *Go away, Pedro. Go back to your prison.* Tiara, he must think of Tiara. She is the solution. God, how she could make him happy. How she could make him unhappy. He is not judging her. If she made him unhappy it was because she herself was miserable. And Rachel, caught in the middle. Her eyes begged them: Don't fight, I need to see you happy.

Happy? Who is happy? Is Adam happy? Is God happy? Are you happy, Karen? Is happiness always born of happiness? As a child, he learned from ancient books that great sadness begets great joy: the Messiah was born on the day of our deepest mourning, says the Talmud. Could he have been misled?

In no way does Karen resemble Tiara. But when Raphael looks at her, it is Tiara's face he sees. Which explains his impulse to kiss Karen. Right now. What would happen if he did? No, he tells himself. Raphael, you must not. They'll lock you up. But what can he do? He has this urge to kiss her painted lips. He tries to reason with himself. But his body won't listen to reason. It has a will of its own. He watches it lean over Karen, reaching out to touch her. He begs it to sit down, he orders it to sit down. But his body couldn't care less about Raphael's orders. His head is close to Karen's, and . . .

The director is standing before them. 'I have been looking for you, Karen.'

Karen stands up, so does Raphael. She leaves with Benedictus and Raphael remains alone. With his clumsiness, his recriminations. He has behaved like a teenager. Is that what he came to the clinic for? *Pedro, my friend, I am weak, weaker than I thought.*

I've been thinking, Pedro, when one is mad, one loves or hates without constraint. When one is mad, one becomes a prison to which the key has been lost. Confronting imprisoned eyes, imprisoned words, one laughs, one cries, one breaks down doors, even those that are open. One climbs mountains, even those deep in the earth's belly. When one is mad, one is everywhere.

That does not mean one is not afraid. Look at me, I'm afraid. Madness is frightening. It frightens those who stand on the threshold not knowing whether to advance or retreat. How wretched they are, those indecisive creatures: they don't know that madness is all around them, that it is like the ocean, infinite; one word too many, one false step, and one is lost.

When one is mad, one rushes toward the unknown. When one is mad, one becomes the unknown. I am afraid of the unknown, Pedro. I am afraid of the stranger inside me, who may or may not be me.

Shrewd like a thousand foxes. Boris is shrewd, that's for sure. Soviet policemen, judges: he has them all in his pocket. Strange, when he appears before them, they relent. Because he is innocent? Not at all. Because he admits his guilt.

'It's good for you to confess your crimes,' he says gravely. 'The earth belongs not to the meek but to the guilty. As does eternity.'

At the clinic, he plays the role of the legendary scapegoat, who long ago, in Judea, bore the sins of the entire people of Israel. Where did he hear that story? Did he stumble upon it in a book? Or had he met a pious Jew in prison, or in the Siberian camps? One of those old men who keeps alive his faith in God, and who would have told him about the solemn Yom Kippur services?

'It's all a game,' says Boris. 'A matter of luck. Why this goat rather than another? Only God has the answer. Why me and not my neighbor? If the prosecutor thinks he knows, he's a fool. He knows no more than anyone else. Perhaps there was something in my name, my file, that caught his attention. Boris, Boris Galperin, that sounds downright suspicious. And there you are: a jot in the margin, and Boris Galperin is no longer free. Only I tricked them. They wanted me to be guilty? Fine. I accommodated them. Guilty of having worked against the regime? Better yet: I told them that I had spent my entire life working against it. Even in my cradle I cried when my dear Communist mother sang her revolutionary lullabies. Later, Grandpa Marx gave me a bellyache. And the famous Little Father of the people made me puke. I used *Pravda* to wrap herring. And *Izvestia* – don't ask. Not for me the official pronouncements of the Party. Not for me the grand economic plans. Long live the anti-Communist utopia! Long live the counterrevolutionary revolution. The various komissars gaped. Never had they come across a criminal the likes of me.

'Names. They wanted, they demanded, names. Fine, I let them have their names, any name that came to my mind. Journalists, artists, celebrities, everybody had his turn. The interrogators couldn't believe their ears. "Is it possible?" they asked. "You were in touch with all these luminaries?" "Of course I was in touch with them. Better than that: I had relationships with them. Do you hear me? Re-la-tion-ships. They gave me their passwords, and I handed over my secrets. We were an outstanding team." The interrogators clamored for facts. And I gave them what they wanted.

'"Yes, I met Nikolai Gregorovitch, the great Nikolai, at the movies. I was with a young whore, he was with an old one. As for Pyotr Sergeyevitch Timoshok, I invited him to dinner. He hardly touched his food, but how he drank!"

'I don't know whether the imbeciles swallowed my nonsense, but they did take everything down in writing, and I signed. They were surely telling themselves: you never know, one day these documents could be useful. Eventually I revealed the identity of my highest superior. The clerk's hand shook as he wrote the name of Lavrenti Beria, the infamous chief of the Soviet police services. The komissars and judges looked panic-stricken. Beria a traitor? Beria a saboteur? One of them shook his finger at me: "What, you swine? You dare soil the reputation of one of the most illustrious defenders of our fatherland?" I was terrified, but I answered: "Honorable citizens and judges, it's one or the other, either permit me to tell the truth, the whole truth, or else send me home." They glanced at one another, then motioned me to continue. They seemed to be saying, You are a liar and a madman, but under Soviet law we must listen to everybody. Of course we know that your rantings have no basis in fact. Lavrenti Beria is a distinguished servant of the Party. But go on anyway. And so I laid it on thicker and thicker.

'I filled one book, five books, with all the monstrous crimes that, together with Beria and his accomplices, I had perpetrated against Stalin and the immortal Socialist fatherland. To seem more convincing, I sobbed as I spoke. I repented, shivering, howling with remorse: "Strike me, honorable judges, I deserve to be punished! Tear me apart, I am worthless! You who are idealists, reduce me to dust, for I allowed myself to be corrupted!"

'The more I carried on, the better my imagination served me. And lo and behold, the scapegoat fleeing toward the desert felt lighter than a feather, lighter than the wind. And the judges were pursuing him, not in order to bring him back, but to discharge upon him their repressed hatred, their cruelty, their panic.

'There I was, running, running in the white sand of the desert, jumping from hill to hill, a trail of uncontrollable laughter in my wake. With my persecutors on my trail, I traversed feasting villages and cities in mourning, dark mountains and valleys in bloom. Now and then I stopped, not to breathe but to receive the sins of people who, having recognized me, rushed to celebrate my mission. Some kneeled down before me, others brought me fruit and honey. I had become a living and necessary God, a celestial power to be worshiped. The judges and komissars observed my triumphs uncomprehendingly. Once, in a tiny village deep in the woods, they tried to question the inhabitants. Outraged, the people pursued them with stones. Nevertheless, they did not give up the chase. My guards had become my prisoners, and they didn't even know it. Like me, because of me, they ended up here. And you know what? You too are here because of me. You don't realize it, but I am the one who runs this place. I, the scapegoat, hold in my hands the fate of all those who live under this roof. I am God. I am God because I am guilty, guiltier than all human beings put together.'

Guilty, he? Well, suspect, perhaps. A native of Russia, he could easily have met Pedro in prison.

'Boris,' says Raphael anxiously, 'in Russia, did you ever meet an exceptional man?'

'Quite a few.'

'A man called Pedro?'

'Pedro? You say Pedro? Of course I knew him. I knew everybody, for everybody was guilty, and I am the God of the guilty. I am the guilty God. Your friend too is guilty, believe me. If you doubt my words, the scapegoat will punish you. Careful, my friend, watch out for the scapegoat's wrath. It is terrible: ask your friend, he knows.'

At the height of his agitation, Boris no longer looks human. He resembles a wild beast ready for the kill. But abruptly his mood changes. He raises his arms and with a radiant expression begins to bless Raphael in the manner of a high priest.

Lidia. The only daughter of Raphael's best friend. Marcus Natanson taught Etruscan civilization; his wife, Alma, German literature. Lidia was the center of their universe. When she came down with a cold, her parents became distraught. When she got an 'A' in French, it was as if they had won the lottery.

Tiara hated them. But Rachel and Lidia got along well. When Tiara walked out on Raphael, Rachel was separated not only from her father but also from her friend. After the divorce, Raphael became a constant guest at the Natansons house. They went everywhere together: plays, concerts, museums.

In his youth, Marcus Natanson could have met Raphael's brother Yoel in a cellar of the NKVD, the Soviet secret police. As for Alma, she could have ended up with Raphael's sisters in the camps.

Fervent Communists, they had belonged to the same cell of the illegal Party in Csodavaros. Marcus was the leader. It was he who had proposed that his cell meet the approaching Red Army. His plan was sensible, its logic indisputable. A Communist's place is in the workers' fatherland, is it not? Since with Jews, especially Jewish Communists, nothing happens without a debate, a passionate and even stormy discussion was bound to take place. And so it did. Would it not be wiser to await instructions from higher up? On the other hand, is it not the duty of a revolutionary to defend his principles? A reference to the Ribbentrop-Molotov pact provoked shouts and incriminations. Typically, this kind of situation precipitated a break. Not this time. 'Pacts,' Marcus said, 'are politics. Communism is truth.' Then he put the issue to a vote. And won. Whereupon Comrade Hersh-the-Redhead declared with a flourish, 'Our unanimous vote reflects the will of the people.' Proud of his victory, Marcus shook everyone's hand and promised that the next meeting would take place in Moscow. Marcus would make discreet arrangements for their departure. Everyone would be notified in the usual manner.

Ascetic, hollow-cheeked, with intense dark eyes, Marcus looked like someone who would be at ease only in the world of books. Yet he was a gifted organizer. Tireless, resourceful, he always knew how to help a comrade in trouble with the police, or a worker who had lost his job, or any other 'victim' of society. He was never ashamed to knock at the doors of the rich, to confront officials, even to interrupt services at the synagogue, if there was an iniquity to be protested. Beloved by the poor, he arbitrated their differences and translated their distress into action.

At sixteen, Marcus was on every police list. Accused of subversive activities, he was arrested and tortured until the head of counterespionage was bribed by the Jewish community and he was released. But he was picked up again whenever the official needed money. Not wanting to be a burden to the community, he moved to a larger city where he thought he could go unnoticed.

A stroke of bad luck. Almost immediately he was rounded up and sent to prison. After escaping, he went back to Csodavaros. 'Here, at least, the authorities know me; they know they cannot break me. Their colleagues elsewhere do not.' He was right. Out of resignation, or perhaps disgust, the head of counterespionage gave up. Marcus was left alone.

During the long winter evenings, as they sat around the warm stove, his comrades would ask him again and again, 'Tell us, how do you manage to resist torture?' Marcus would scold them: 'What's wrong with you? Must you speak of that?' Alma, the most stubborn of all, would needle him: 'What if I'm arrested? Don't you think I should know what to do?' He didn't answer. Was he in love with her? His comrades thought so, but he denied it. The more they insisted, the more he protested. But it was all true: he liked the way she listened, the way she laughed.

And Alma, did she love him? She loved them all. She looked at all the boys with such tenderness that each was convinced that she loved only him. Except Marcus. He was convinced of the opposite.

Years later, when Marcus returned to Csodavaros from Siberia, he found Alma, who had survived the Polish death camps. The two embraced. They were all that remained of their community.

Marcus had spent almost ten years in the Kolyma. Alma, whose parents would not let her go to Soviet Russia, had shared the fate of most of the Jews of the region. She had been sent first to Birkenau, then to Ravensbrück. The last months of the ordeal she spent in Belsen.

In the first days and weeks after the war, they spoke ceaselessly about the nightmare. Then one day they vowed never to speak of it again. They married, emigrated to the United States, and began their studies at the university where Raphael was an instructor.

Though it was never discussed, Raphael was keenly aware of the Natansons' past. Only once had Marcus let his defenses down. It was when Tiara was in the hospital. Raphael was helping Alma clear the table. Rachel and Lidia were playing in the next room. Marcus was in his favorite armchair near the window, stuffing his pipe. Suddenly, Alma asked how things were with Tiara. He lied: 'Everything will be fine.' Marcus turned to look at him. 'I don't believe you.' Seeing Raphael's dismay, he added, 'When somebody tells me everything will be fine, I know that things couldn't be worse.' Lighting his pipe, he said to Raphael, 'We are your friends. I am not saying that we are entitled to know, only that we are concerned.' Overcoming his reticence, Raphael revealed that Tiara was pregnant and that she did not want the child. 'You and Tiara are dear to us,' Marcus went on, 'You do know that.' He exhaled and watched a few puffs of smoke dance in the air. 'Sometimes I wonder,' he continued, 'if I don't bring bad luck to my friends. Of our entire group, only Alma and I survived.' 'Why such a black mood?' asked Raphael. 'Things are going well for you, aren't they?' Neither Marcus nor Alma responded. But Marcus's eyes changed color. That's the kind of eyes he had. They could explain everything from the origin of species to the secret of death. No wonder so many women on campus were after him. One young instructor admitted it: Those eyes made her feel as if she were being made love to on a bed of clouds.

'Listen, Raphael,' said Marcus. But Raphael was no longer listening. He was thinking of Tiara. He loved Tiara. He loved his wife, he loved the mother of his child. But he could not speak of it, not even to Marcus and Alma, which added to his sadness.

They could never understand that for him love was still a mystical experience. When he met Tiara, he felt that their lives meshed completely, that there had been no woman before her. And now Tiara was in the hospital, untying the bonds between them forever.

At eighteen, Lidia entered a small liberal arts college in northern New Jersey. She came home every Friday for Shabbat dinner with her parents. The Natansons were not especially religious, but were intent on keeping the Jewish tradition alive. On Friday nights they sang together, and sometimes Raphael joined in. Hasidic melodies, ancient prayers set to music: the Queen of Shabbat triumphed in heaven and on earth.

One rainy Friday in April, Lidia was late coming home. What could have happened to her? An accident? Ten hypotheses, each worse than the next, ran through their heads. She had been hit by a car, attacked by a maniac, abducted by a kidnapper. Marcus phoned the college. Of course they knew nothing.

'There is only one thing to do,' announced Raphael, who couldn't bear his friends' distress. 'I'll drive out to the campus and call you from there.'

The roads were slick, cars were skidding left and right. The bridge was jammed. A forty-five-minute trip took Raphael two hours. He stopped to call Marcus and Alma from the road.

'Any news?'

'Nothing,' said Marcus. 'We're sick with worry.'

'Be patient. I'll be on campus in a few minutes.'

Naturally, all the offices were closed. Whom could he ask for information? He entered one of the buildings. There was a light at the end of a hallway and he walked toward it. When Raphael opened the door he found himself in the middle of Friday night services. The room was the meeting place of Hillel, the Jewish student organization. A few dozen students were gathered around a cantor who was chanting the traditional melodies. When services ended, the cantor went over to the visitor. 'Can I help you?'

'I'm looking for a friend, Lidia Natanson.'

The cantor's face darkened. He beckoned to a few students to come closer, and explained the visitor's purpose. One of the girls murmured, 'Lidia . . . Poor Lidia.'

Soon Raphael was brought up-to-date. For many weeks now, Lidia had been associating with a group of young people from a commune who were under the influence of an authoritarian 'guru'.

'But her parents know nothing of this,' said Raphael.

'Of course not,' they said.

Raphael called the Natansons. 'Listen, she's alive and well.'

'But where is she?' cried Marcus.

'Not with me, I'm afraid. I'll explain when I get back.'

A student was waiting at a discreet distance while Raphael spoke on the phone. When he hung up, the young man approached and said:

'I want to talk to you about Lidia. I like her, I may even love her. But I must tell you that she is living a lie.'

'What is your name?'

'Roman. I am a philosophy student.'

'Do you know where the commune is located?'

'I have an idea. But I'm sure I can get you exact directions.'

Raphael gave him his number and asked him to call the first instant he could.

In the meantime, the rain had let up. Raphael was back at the Natansons' in less than an hour. Before he could speak, Alma cried, 'Where's Lidia? Is she all right?'

'Yes and no.'

Forcing himself to adopt a neutral tone, he reported what he had found out.

'Our Lidia?' stammered Alma. 'I refuse to believe it.'

'We are so close,' added Marcus. 'Why didn't she say something?'

'There must be a mistake,' said Alma. 'That's it . . . A case of mistaken identity.'

'I'm sorry,' said Raphael.

'I don't believe it,' said Alma. 'Lidia would never leave us for a commune! It's totally unlike her.'

Marcus shook his head sadly and whispered, 'To give up Moses for some guru . . . My poor little Lidia.'

Raphael will never forget that Friday night. A family torn apart. That Shabbat, the Angels of Peace had brought something other than peace: grief, shame, remorse. 'I must not cry,' a crying Alma repeated again and again. Why are we being punished? What did we do? Marcus asked himself.

Alma served dinner. It was left untouched. After dinner, they usually went to the living room to discuss faculty promotions and intrigues, foreign affairs: Israel, Russian Jews. Not this time. Lidia's absence eclipsed everything else. Raphael summed up the situation as optimistically as he could.

'Listen, Lidia is alive, and I will soon know where she is. When I do, I'll go speak to her. Trust me, there is every reason to hope.'

Marcus was pale. His eyes seemed to follow distant images. His face showed raw pain as he began to speak.

'I remember,' he said, struggling with his emotions, 'in my town there was a young Jewish girl from a good family who fell in love with a Pole, a Christian doctor she had met at the university. Her name was Reizele Harziger. Her father, Melekh Harziger, was a merchant, a pious man, and a Talmudic scholar. People envied him his children as much as his wealth. They were handsome and well brought up. The boys studied at the yeshiva, the girls played the piano. Their house was bright, spacious, welcoming. The cooks had orders never to turn anyone away with an empty stomach. I remember the orchard in back of their courtyard. As a child I went there to pick cherries and plums. I remember the happy little girl who accompanied us. Reizele had black pigtails that fell over her shoulders. Her father adored her. There were times when he came home just to stroke her hair or hold her hand in his. He bought her the most beautiful dresses, the most expensive toys; he promised her the most desirable bridegroom in town. But Reizele thought her father would give her even more than that: his consent to her marriage to the young Polish doctor.

'One evening at the dinner table, she announced her wedding plans. Her mother began to sob, her father fainted. During the weeks that followed, the house resounded with laments. "Reizele, you are killing us," moaned her mother. "You are covering us with shame," cried her brothers and sisters. Melekh promised his rabbi that he would build him a new House of Study if he would only bring his daughter back to reason. The mother threw herself onto the graves of the rabbis, imploring them to intercede in heaven on their behalf.

'In a Hasidic *shtibl*, ten men recited psalms from morning till night. One uncle advised the distraught father to distribute one-tenth of his wealth to the poor, another wrote to Jerusalem asking that a plea be inserted into the cracks of the Wall. The support of heavenly and earthly powers was solicited. But Reizele was stubborn: "If you really loved me, you would love whomever I love."

'Private discussions, family councils, arguments based on faith, counterarguments based on emotion. Nevertheless, Reizele announced her decision to wed in the spring.

'On her wedding day, church bells rang out, calling Christians to come and rejoice with the young couple. At that very moment, the entire Jewish community was filing through the Harzigers' house to console them.

'Harziger and his wife, surrounded by their sons and daughters, were sitting on low stools in observance of the laws of mourning. Within one year, he was dead and his wife had gone mad. The remaining members of the family perished in the camps. As for Reizele, I don't know whether she achieved happiness or what ultimately happened to her. I do know that she asked permission to attend her father's funeral, and that it was not given.'

Marcus fell silent. Alma was weeping. Raphael was going to say something but changed his mind.

'It remains to be seen whether Lidia is still my daughter,' concluded Marcus.

'Don't say that,' begged Alma. 'She'll come home. I know she'll come home.'

'I think you're right,' said Raphael. 'She'll come home. I'll bring her home. I promise.'

Early Sunday morning, he received Roman's call. He had all the necessary information.

The Village of Felicity, on Long Island, resembled a military camp. It was off limits to strangers; to enter, one had to obtain a pass from the security office.

Raphael confronted a barrage of questions:

'Who are you looking for? Why? Who sent you?'

He was forced to open his briefcase, which the guard rummaged through at great length. When he finished at last, he directed Raphael to the central office, where he would be received by the Brother Director. Who made him wait. The waiting room was spartan: bare walls, bare table, bare floor. Through a small round window, the only one, Raphael had a view of a tranquil, well-tended garden of flowerbeds bordering a fountain. A weirdly calculated peace hung over the place.

Suddenly, a voice made him jump: 'I am Patra, the Brother Director of this village.' Dressed in white, head slightly inclined, palms touching in the traditional greeting, he scrutinized the visitor. 'How can I be of service to you?'

'The daughter of a friend is here. I wish to speak to her.'

'What is her name?'

'Lidia. Lidia Natanson.'

'Lidia, Lidia . . . That name means nothing to me. You see, our brothers and sisters relinquish their names when they come into our family. That is the rule.' There ensued a discourse on the meaninglessness of names.

Raphael interrupted him. 'Never mind all that. Mysticism is my field.'

'What, you, a mystic?' asked the Brother Director with a broad smile. 'In that case . . .'

'I am not a mystic; I teach mystical traditions, among others. But my coming here has nothing to do with mysticism. I am here to see Lidia Natanson. If you prevent me from seeing her, your next visitor will be a police officer. By the way, I thought it prudent to inform the police of my visit here.'

The Brother Director feigned dismay:

'Threats? From the mouth of a professor of mysticism? Not nice, not nice at all. You want to see Lidia Natanson? All right, let's go find her, shall we?'

Raphael followed the Brother Director outside into the garden, which led into a larger garden, bordered with trees. Under a huge oak, men and women swathed in colored sheets appeared to be in a state of prayer. At regular intervals, an emaciated man with a birdlike face and spectacles chanted words that made no sense to Raphael.

'Oh sun of my blood, rise and discover a sign of your sign.'

Then they all began to clap and to emit shrill bursts of laughter and shouts of joy. Raphael's eyes searched for Lidia but did not find her in the mesmerized group, who saw and heard only the Guide of Dawn.

Before Raphael could say anything, the Brother Director placed a finger over his lips: the interdiction was absolute. It was forbidden to disturb the Guide and his disciples while they were in a state of trance. An interruption – he whispered to Raphael – could result in death.

The session lasted a full half-hour. It was a beautiful spring day, cool, sunny. Perfect for transcendental experiments. The initiated locked hands, forming a vibrant circle around their Guide, who rocked from side to side as he chanted:

'Forget the I so as to attain the plenitude of the Being. Forget the I. And the god in me will be reborn in oblivion . . .'

His disciples followed his vaguely erotic movements, shouting incoherently, bending down to the damp earth. To Raphael, it looked like a primitive rite celebrating the union of gods.

'Look,' whispered the Brother Director in the visitor's ear. 'A sacred alliance is being forged before your eyes. All these bodies, all these souls, will become one as God is one; don't you wish you could elevate yourself toward Him?'

'I have only one wish: to see Lidia Natanson.'

The session was coming to an end. Suddenly the disciples seemed paralyzed, struck by lightning. Heads turned skyward, hands folded on their knees, they waited patiently for the Guide of Dawn to rise and bless them. Which in time he did.

'May the grace of the eternal void go through you like a tamed spirit crossing the forest of illusion . . . may the eye of infinite space open for you as the tree opens its foliage to the burning dew.'

As for Raphael, he was burning with rage.

Only when the disciples began to disperse did Raphael see Lidia. The girl was wrapped in a white sari. Wan and frail, her eyes wide with fear, she was almost unrecognizable. When she saw Raphael she looked away.

'Sister Ishamar,' said the Brother Director, 'you have a visitor.'

Raphael felt a wave of tenderness and pity for her. He wished he could take her into his arms as he had when she was a little girl, and carry her away, as far away as possible from this accursed place.

'Thank you for coming,' said Lidia weakly. 'May the light of midnight be your reward. May the grace of the wandering bird be your haven.'

Poor Lidia, she was expressing herself like her guide. Was it because the Brother Director was present? Raphael politely requested to be left alone with her. Confident of his hold on Lidia, the Brother Director stepped aside.

'Lidia,' said Raphael, reaching for her hand, 'please come home. Your parents are taking this very badly. You are all they have, you know that.'

'I know I am hurting them. But in time the hurt will transform itself into something holy. Once upon a time I lived inside a being that hurt me. Not anymore. What has happened to me will happen to my parents as well. I know you are surprised by what I am saying; you cannot understand that thanks to our Guide of Dawn I have found serenity.'

A smile flickered across the Brother Director's face. He hadn't missed a word of their conversation. If only I could strangle him, thought Raphael. Break his neck.

'Lidia,' he whispered, 'I do understand. You want to shed your troubles . . . renew yourself . . . redefine yourself. But why must you hurt your parents in the process? They love you. They'll respect your need to experiment. Why exclude them? Why reject them? Try to imagine their lives without you, try to imagine their grief.'

Lidia appeared to be listening, but there was no evidence of Raphael's words having reached her. Still, he did not give up.

'They think it's their fault, Lidia. Have mercy on them.'

'I pity them. I pity the whole world. Our Guide of the Dawn has opened my heart to pity. I pity the pilgrims lost in the desert. And the shepherds running after their flock. And the starving children. And the slaughtered sheep. I pity the dry leaves that fall to the ground. And the clouds that vanish. Believe me, my friend, not only am I capable of pity, but mine is as vast as the universe.'

There was nothing more to be said.

'All right, Lidia. I'll leave you now. Is there anything you'd like me to tell your parents?'

She stared at him, an unnatural gleam in her eyes.

'Tell them that their daughter suffered when she was their daughter; she no longer suffers. She has awakened from a long sleep. And now her soul lives in the soul of the earth and swims in the soul of the sea.'

Abruptly, she bowed and left. The next moment, the Brother Director was at Raphael's side:

'Ishamar has a great soul. We are proud of her. The Guide of Dawn predicts for her a bright and fruitful eternity.'

Raphael pretended not to hear. Sick at heart, he left the 'Village' as one leaves a prison: without looking back.

'She'll return,' said Alma, trying to convince herself.

Raphael was not so sure. The Village of Felicity was a jail whose inmates believed it was paradise.

'I should have gone with you,' said Marcus.

Soon after, he fell ill. Raphael wired Lidia to come home. Her answer too was in the form of a telegram: 'Greetings to my father, who dances in the vineyard with open palms.'

'If I were devout,' said Marcus, 'I would tear my clothes in mourning as Harziger once did.'

Raphael tried to comfort his friend:

'Don't, Marcus. Lidia did not convert. This may just be a phase.'

Instead of arguing, Marcus began studying the Jewish laws of mourning: the torn garments, the interdiction to shave or listen to music, the custom of leaving the door ajar so that those wishing to console the mourner may enter without knocking.

A few weeks later, Raphael understood Marcus's sudden interest in mourning: he had died in his sleep.

Another telegram to Lidia. Alma Natanson had been right: Lidia did come home.

But it was too late.

Rachel, my beloved daughter,

I am writing to you from a lovely spot in the mountains. The sun is shining, the birds are singing, the trees are in bloom. I can see you through the branches, capturing the golden rays. You are laughing and I love to see you laugh.

I have been here for several weeks now on an unusual assignment. I am meeting some extraordinary people, characters from the Bible. We have, dwelling among us, none other than Cain, Abraham, and Joseph. And guess what, even the Messiah! Can you imagine? I'll tell you more about it when I see you.

And you, my beautiful Rachel, what are you doing? Are you having a good vacation? Are you having fun? . . .

God, how I miss her, Pedro. Tiara knew I loved the name Rachel. That's why she insisted on calling her Rita. To annoy me. She knew how much importance I attach to names. But Tiara never missed a chance to vex me. 'Rachel, Rachel, I couldn't care less about that name. Rachel is for the Bible, not for the twentieth century. My daughter's name is Rita, and that's that. If you don't like it, go find yourself another woman and let her make you a Rachel!' I kept quiet, Pedro. You taught me silence . . . How did we ever reach this point?

⋆

A memory:

'I'm pregnant,' Tiara announced.

How could Raphael describe the warmth that enveloped him? What name could he give it? Happiness. Joy. Pride. A little anguish, no doubt. He embraced his wife. She pushed him away.

'What's wrong, Tiara? You should be happy. Rachel needs company,' Raphael told her.

'Happy?' she shrieked. 'Happy about what? What's good for you is not necessarily good for me. I am too old for this, too old to be a mother again.'

Tiara was having a tantrum. Her delicate features were twisted, her hair was wild. She was out of control. If he didn't watch out, she would attack him. And, incorrigible romantic that he was, he remembered the night, six weeks ago – or was it seven? – when he made love to her passionately, desperately. Half asleep, she had drawn him toward her and had held him close. Naively, at that moment, he thought that she loved him too . . .

'I'll never let you touch me again,' she screamed. 'One child is enough. Anyway, you disgust me. Go away.'

Raphael struggled to overcome his feelings. He spoke to her tenderly, lovingly, of all they had together: their child, their future. He promised to spend more time with her, to take her to the beach, to the mountains; to make more money, to buy a country house . . .

She replied vindictively:

'How do you plan to do all this? On your shabby little professor's salary? Of all the wretched men I've known, you are the most wretched: you cling to misery as it clings to you. Some husband and father you make!'

The sadness that came over Raphael was definitive. Finally he understood: his wife hated him. He wished he knew why.

Hesitantly, he asked her. She responded by locking herself in the bathroom.

Raphael had to lean against a table for support. He felt faint, nauseous. A fiendish hand was crushing him. A nightmare, he told himself. It must be a nightmare. After all, Tiara is my wife. We shared unique experiences, laughed and cried for the same reasons. We were so close to one another. Or were we? Could I have been so blind? Was she just a liar? An actress? Was she insane? That's it, he thought. This must be a passing madness. Maybe such things happen to pregnant women of her age. He had better get her to a doctor. She may need medication. He and Rachel will take care of her. The Natansons will help. Tiara will recover. She will once again be his wife, the mother of his children. Still, he wondered: Was she really pregnant? What if this were another one of her games, the kind she sometimes played to torment him? To warn him not to take her for granted.

Raphael dragged himself to the kitchen, poured himself a glass of cold water, gulped it down. Then he washed his face. Now he felt better. He knocked on the bathroom door: Tiara did not answer. He knocked harder: she still did not answer. What was she doing? Raphael panicked. Could she be taking her life? He pounded on the door, ready to smash it down if need be. At last she answered. 'Go away,' she screamed. 'I don't want to see you; I don't ever want to see you again.'

'Tiara, what are you doing in there?'

'None of your business.'

'I'm worried about you.'

'Go away.'

'Should I call a doctor?'

'Just go away.'

Raphael looked at his watch. It was 8:30 A.M. on a Monday in February. He suddenly remembered that he had a class. He must hurry. His students would worry. They knew how punctual he was . . . He could remember nothing, not even what he was supposed to teach. He was totally confused: he must leave, but he could not. He could not leave Tiara, who might be pregnant, who might be suicidal. He could not leave Tiara, who hated him. His students were waiting for him but he resumed his vigil in front of the bathroom.

As he sat there, he kept glancing at his watch. He imagined his students shifting in their seats. He saw their anxious faces. George, the nice young man from South Carolina, went to the office to inquire: Is the professor ill? Has he been called out of town? Raphael saw Rose, the department secretary, shaking her head: No, she had no idea why Professor Lipkin was late. George said: He's never done this before. We must try to reach him. Rose dialed his number. The phone rang. He must get up, he knew he must get up, he must answer, but he did not. He was afraid to leave his post. Tiara might escape, never to return.

The phone kept ringing. That's enough, Rose! Stop! Finally, silence. In an instant the phone rang again. Rose probably thought she had dialed a wrong number. No, she had not dialed a wrong number. She let it ring and ring until his head was bursting.

'Answer,' screamed Tiara.

Raphael didn't feel like answering. Besides, what would he say to Rose: that Tiara is pregnant? That she hates him? That she wants to kill herself? That she is going mad?

'For God's sake, answer,' screamed Tiara, even louder this time.

'Okay, okay.' He rushed to the kitchen, picked up the phone. Too late. Rose had given up. He could hear her telling the students: I don't understand, there's no answer. I hope nothing has happened to him, said George. Don't worry, George, I'll be all right. Rose decided to call the Natansons. No answer there either. God, what if something has happened to him, said George. Don't worry, George, nothing has happened to me, nothing but a few small mishaps, nothing to worry about. My wife is going mad, my family is coming apart, my life is ruined, that's all.

'Who was it?' screamed Tiara.

'Nobody,' he said. 'They hung up.'

'Typical,' said Tiara.

He was silent. There was nothing left to say.

'My father sent me to my death. Knowingly. A terrible accusation, but true. I swear it on my head and his. I am Joseph, his son, and he hates me. I don't know why.

'He loved my mother, that is well known. He worked fourteen long years for his uncle to win her as his bride. When my mother gave birth to me, he was ecstatic. You don't believe me? Read the Bible, it's all there. He spoiled me, he doted on me. My older brothers could not help but be jealous. Those fools! Couldn't they see that it was all a pretense? I never figured out why, but my father had a grudge against me. He saw to it that my brothers hated and excluded me . . .'

Small and wiry, Joseph gesticulates wildly. He behaves like a man possessed.

Listening to him, Raphael remembers his own father, his boundless love for his children. And the fact that Aharon was always careful not to favor one child over another.

Joseph evokes a memory of his own:

'A warm Saturday afternoon. My father, a holy book open on the table before him, seemed to be dozing. As I tiptoed toward him, he opened his eyes and began to mutter incoherently. "Tell me," he said, "am I awake or am I dreaming?"

"Father, you're awake, you're looking at me." He shrugged. "Well, you *could* be in my dream."

'Suddenly, his face looked distorted. When I asked if he was in pain, he did not answer. Was he having a heart attack? I was about to run for help when I heard him speak as if in a trance. These were his words: "I find myself in a strange land," he said. "A land inhabited by demons. I don't know what I did to get here, but I know that in order to leave I must invent a story. I don't eat, I don't sleep. Instead, I try to remember the stories learned or read since my childhood. I begin to weep, while the demons laugh. The more they laugh, the more I cry. I beg them to let me go. They answer me with a great roar of laughter. An old demon tells me: 'You are wrong to curse us; it is not our fault that we cannot weep. We would love to be able to shed tears, but we cannot.' Then he winks at me as if we were accomplices, as if we were sharing a secret and he were pledging not to betray it. When I look at him again he seems familiar. With a start, I recognize the old demon; he is not old and he is not a demon. He is my lost son. He speaks to me: 'You wish to leave, old man; you want to go home. Nothing could be easier. Just tell us the story of your lost son, we don't know it.' But I cannot do that, for fear of harming my son. So I bow my head in silence. Tears are burning my cheeks. I ache, I ache terribly, and I don't know what to do." '

Raphael watches Joseph as he circles the room in a frenzy. Why did he tell him this story? Was it to convince Raphael that his father loved him after all? Or was he trying to convince himself? To judge from his state, he remains convinced that his father is his mortal enemy.

Zelig's head is tilted skyward, as if he were searching for something. Don't ask him for what; he won't tell you. Raphael has asked him once, ten times; he makes believe he doesn't hear. Maybe he doesn't.

All day long and sometimes late into the night, Zelig stands in the garden, or at his window, staring up at the stars. The stars are his only interest. He is indifferent to everything else – inside or outside the clinic.

He has no friends among the staff, nor among the patients. Perhaps because he refuses to acknowledge other people's existence. Nothing exists for him but the sky.

Sometimes he seems to be telling it stories. They must be sad stories, for he often appears to be crying. One day, he seems so sad that Raphael walks over to him and puts his arm on his shoulder. Then he realizes that Zelig is not crying at all, but trembling, trembling from head to toe. Raphael leaves without a word, not wanting to disturb him.

Raphael is fascinated by this patient, who seems different from the others. He does not live in Biblical times, does not take himself for Cain or Joseph. A gentle man, he harms no one, nor has he ever tried to harm himself. What is he seeking? His file gives no clue. It discloses a 'normal' childhood in Chicago, a sheltered adolescence, marriage at twenty-one to a friend of his sister's, work in real estate for his father-in-law. No problems until the day his wife accused him of being in the clouds. 'I'm sorry, that's how I am,' he replied. 'I can't help it. You see, people think the sky is empty but I know it's not. Since no one else seems to care, I've taken it upon myself to find out who or what is there.' At first his wife had laughed the whole thing off. But Zelig's contemplation of the clouds was taking more and more of his time. He began to neglect his affairs. Then his wife. Not only that, but he became a menace to himself and others, running into walls, crashing into furniture, getting in the way of bicycles. One day he fainted in the street. The doctor who examined him called in a psychiatrist.

It all reminds Raphael of a tale by Rabbi Nahman of Bratslav: the tale of a prince who, believing himself to be a turkey, refused to eat with his family. A wise man, seeking to heal him, decided he too would claim to be a turkey. So he joined the prince beneath the table. The two became friends, and the prince recovered.

Could he not do the same? Raphael wonders. Could he not also probe the mysteries of the skies? One day, he follows Zelig into the garden, his eyes fixed on the transparent blue sky. Zelig glances at him suspiciously. Raphael pretends not to notice; the celestial situation is too absorbing. One hour goes by, then two. Fortunately, he is capable of intense concentration. If he can spend twelve hours on an ancient text, he should also be able to devote a few hours to a sliver of sky.

When dusk falls, he leaves the garden, walking backward, his eyes glued to the sky. The next day he resumes his post. Zelig seems even more disconcerted than before: Who is this intruder? Raphael continues to show no interest in him. The following day, Zelig confronts him. 'Why are you watching me?' Raphael takes no notice. 'Why are you watching me?' Raphael takes no notice. 'Why are you spying on me? Who are you? What do you want from me?' Raphael turns a deaf ear. Now it is Zelig who watches him. At the end of one hour, Raphael allows himself a sigh. Zelig is all ears. 'Oh, yes,' says Raphael in a half-whisper, 'they are all there.' The truth is, he has uttered these words without really knowing why. But Zelig understands, Zelig knows. He takes a step toward Raphael. 'So you see them too, don't you? You see them as I see them.' Raphael answers, 'Yes, they are all there; look, there they are.'

And so they become allies. As in the Hasidic tale, they take their meals together, go out into the garden together, scrutinize the sky, interrogate it with their eyes, and communicate their findings to one another. All this is fine, but Raphael is still baffled. He knows how to play the game, but this cannot go on indefinitely. Raphael feels that Zelig will soon reveal himself. When he finally does, Raphael congratulates himself, feels like shouting with joy. He has prevailed. But as soon as Zelig speaks, as soon as Raphael grasps the meaning of his words, his joy deserts him.

'The sky is beautiful,' says Zelig, 'oh, how beautiful it is, beautiful like a cemetery; it is the most beautiful cemetery in the world . . . majestic . . . spectacular . . . Look over there, on the left: a gathering of mute men and women; they are listening to a mute speaker . . .'

Like Zelig, Raphael sees a trail of glittering stars set like gravestones in a velvet sky. He sees dead men and women entranced by a mute speaker. No, the speaker is not mute, the speaker is Zelig. I am mad, Raphael thinks. As mad as he.

Zelig is trembling again:

'I know people think I have lost my mind. They probably think the same of you. Why? Because we are both seeking, seeking our dead. I've been at it for years. Vanished, all of them. In one night. In the time it takes God to frown, they were gone. Emptied, the towns of Poland. Evacuated, the villages of Hungary. Erased, the hamlets of Lithuania. Jews had lived there for centuries, until the lethal wind blew. All this I learned from my favorite uncle, who came back from there. He witnessed that which God Himself did not wish to see. A sweet, quiet man, my uncle would only smile sadly when people asked him what he had seen. He wanted them to understand his sadness, his silences. He liked me because I, for one, tried to understand. I began to devour books and documents. But the more I learned, the less I understood. The killings, the massacres, they were familiar to me; our history is filled with them. But this crime was different. This was an entirely new crime: an absolute crime. Absolute, since the killers made the corpses disappear. For the first time in our history, the victims could not even be buried. Six million human beings, that's a whole country, a nation. After all, they couldn't have been erased like a typographical error. Or could they?

'And so I began to search. First, I tried the cemeteries. I must have visited every cemetery in Europe, small ones, large ones, rich and poor ones. Ones that are known and others that are not. I found nothing. I explored wastelands, mountains, forests: still nothing. Yes, I discovered mass graves here and there, vast pits covered with lime and ashes. But where were all the other corpses? Eventually I came up with a theory: they must all have gone to heaven. I glanced up at the sky. My heart began to pound: I was right. There they were; there they remain.'

It has been a while since Zelig stopped trembling. But his delivery is halting. He begins a sentence and interrupts himself as if he were afraid of where it will lead.

'Look, over there. An old man holding his grandson's hand . . . A woman with her little girl . . . They too are holding hands . . . And there, to the left, a man is searching for his lost children . . . A rabbi is summoning his disciples . . . And coming toward us, a procession of adolescents, their eyes riveted to a flaming mountain . . . Wait a minute. This is strange . . .'

A sense of foreboding comes over Raphael, but he is determined to hear Zelig out.

'How strange,' says Zelig. 'I see you. I don't mean here . . . I mean up there. With them . . .'

'Who are you?' the patient asks, waving his hand dismissively.

'Raphael Lipkin. And you?'

'You don't know who I am?'

'Well . . . no . . .'

'That's a good one. You see me as I see you, and you don't know who I am.'

'I'm sorry, but . . .'

'But what? They must have told you that I am the Messiah.'

In his early thirties, tall, gaunt, with a straggly beard, he is squatting on the floor and speaking to Raphael earnestly:

'Don't worry. I'll save you anyway. I'll even save those who refuse to be saved. In fact, I'll save them first. That is my mission. The Lord entrusted me with it. He has several saviors, the Lord. One takes care of wise men, the other of fools. The Messiah of the Just lives next door. I'm the Messiah of the Wicked. Thieves and killers come to me for salvation.'

Once again, Raphael is surprised by the logic inherent in madness. Come to think of it, why would there be a savior for the just but none for the damned? Is the need of the wicked not greater?

Long ago in Rovidok, the old madman had told him that the Messiah waited for the call with painful impatience. 'God cannot free man,' he said. 'It is man alone who must summon the savior from his palace or prison, to come to the rescue of mankind. But what if, in his impatience, the savior loses his mind? What then? If he no longer knows who he is or what his mission is, what then . . .?'

If the wicked have their Messiah and the just have theirs, why wouldn't there be a Messiah for madmen? This patient holds a special fascination for Raphael. Since childhood, he has loved messianic tales. Mysticism intrigues him because of the Messiah's role in it. He loves the philosophical implications: the coming of the Messiah as the conclusion of history, the sublimation of the wait. Even his relationship to Pedro is linked to his love for the Messiah. He became attached to Pedro because he recognized in him certain messianic traits: an aura of mystery, the breadth of his humanism, the depth of his silences.

'They'll tell you many things about me,' said the patient. 'They are all true. They'll tell you that I'm sick; I am. That I'm demented; I am. As for me, I tell you that I am the Messiah. I can see you don't believe me. Skepticism is written all over your face.'

In fact, Raphael has consulted his file and thus knows his history. The son of a Protestant minister, he had, just before finishing his studies in theology at Princeton, fallen under the influence of a pseudo-mystical sect. At his initiation, he experimented with a hallucinogenic drug. The next week was one of agonizing delirium. Day after day, he crouched in a corner of his room. Nightmarish thoughts pierced his head, toxic air tore through his lungs. One night, he ran out of his dormitory, climbed to the roof, and tried to jump. To the psychiatrist who came to administer tranquilizers, he explained that he had returned from heaven with a mission to save mankind.

'I know,' says the patient. 'You think I'm lying. You think I'm making it all up. Go ahead, tell me I'm delirious. You won't be the first or the last. Besides, you'll be doing me a favor. The more I suffer, the closer I am to my goal. Where would Christ be without his suffering? Where would Jesus, son of Joseph and Mary, be without his death? And I, where would I be if I were happy?'

'You're right,' says Raphael. 'The Messiah is never happy.'

'Bravo!' shouts the patient. 'But wait a minute, who told you that? Don't tell me you are his confidant.'

'No, my friend. You are the only one he trusts.'

They settle into two chairs. The patient peers at him. 'Tell me, what do you know about the Messiah?'

'Not much.'

'That's not the way it looks to me. Please, I beg of you, tell me all you know.'

Raphael is moved by the urgency of his request. 'I don't know if I told you, but I am a Jew.'

'A Jew! I should have guessed! You're the only people who take the Messiah seriously! Go on, I'm listening.'

And so Raphael begins to speak. Of the difference between the mystery of the beginning and that of the end. Of God and the *Shekhina*. Of the ten *Sephirot*. Of the perils of forbidden knowledge. He tells him the mystical story of the four sages who entered the orchard.

'More,' says the patient.

Raphael obliges, but he stops in mid-sentence. I really must be going mad, he thinks, to be explaining Jewish mysticism to a man who takes himself for the Messiah.

'More,' urges the patient.

And Raphael does tell him more.

'In my tradition, the Messiah is anonymous,' he says. 'Our sources put greater emphasis on messianic times than on the Messiah's personality. For us, the wait is more important than the wish to be the Messiah.'

'No wonder you endure so many maledictions! How naive of you! How do you expect him to come, if none of you aspires to be him?'

Smiling, Raphael says, 'Our aim is to prepare the way for him. To open doors for him.'

'Incredible how little ambition you Jews have!'

Raphael watches as the patient gets up and restlessly moves around the room.

'Why is it not as ambitious,' Raphael asks him, 'to bring the Messiah as to become the Messiah? When I was a child, my parents gave me a blessing: that I might live long enough to witness the coming of the Messiah.'

'Well, their blessing has been realized! Here you are in the presence of the Messiah . . . Have you nothing to say? You repudiate me just as your people repudiated Christ? Aren't you afraid of retribution? Never mind, I'll save you in spite of yourself.'

Raphael is at a loss. 'Why don't you sit down?' he urges.

Absently, the patient complies and goes on:

'Sometimes I envy my colleague, the Messiah of the Just. His kingdom is filled with beauty and holiness, mine is ugly and twisted. His radiates joy, mine is steeped in violence. And yet . . .'

And yet, thinks Raphael, he is mad. And yet, he wants to save the world.

What exactly did I expect to find here in this clinic, Pedro? My stolen memories? My hidden wounds? I am neither ill nor a healer. Psychiatry interests me only insofar as it coincides with literature. Hamlet paranoid? Faust schizophrenic? If I could, I would ask Lear to write a play on Shakespeare. To me, Raskolnikov's opinion of Dostoevsky is no less valid than Fyodor the Epileptic's opinion of Raskolnikov. No, psychiatry as an end never engaged me. I've always believed that a great novelist is able to see the entanglements of the human soul better than any psychiatrist. And now, here I am in alien territory, surrounded by psychiatrists and their patients. In truth, Pedro, this is turning out to be a strange vacation . . .

Long ago, when Raphael was still married, he would get into the car with his small family and venture forth: to the Grand Canyon, Yellowstone, the coast of Maine. Rachel loved to travel. She loved the motels, the restaurants. She loved the unknown. Since the divorce, Raphael hasn't known what to do with his vacations. They have become a burden. In the beginning, he stayed with the Natansons at their cottage near the beach. He played with Lidia, flying kites with her, building sand castles, racing her in the water. Playing with her made him happy, but also sad: it reminded him of Rachel, who had stayed with her mother. Perhaps that was why, the following summer, he decided against spending it with the Natansons. It was easier to withdraw, keep to himself, stay close to the campus. His motherly housekeeper admonished him: 'Professor,' she said with concern, 'you should . . .' 'I should what?' 'Maybe you should . . .' Isn't it incredible, thought Raphael, how many people leave their sentences unfinished? Still, he knew what advice she wanted to give him: to go out and have a good time, to find a woman, to make a new life. He appreciated the advice, but all he wanted was peace.

Raphael was preparing himself to go on another solitary vacation when, late one night in May, there came the phone call that induced him to move into the clinic. He had been busy correcting a paper on comparative asceticism when the phone rang, breaking his concentration. Who could it be? No student would dare disturb him at that hour. A colleague? Among the faculty, Marcus had been his only close friend. And now he was gone. Rachel then? Tiara, about Rachel? Anxiously, he picked up the receiver:

'Is this Professor Lipkin?'

'Yes. Who is this?'

'Never mind. I'd like to speak to you about . . .'

The voice was cold, unfamiliar, the speech slightly accented.

'Unless you tell me who you are, I . . .'

'This is not about me, Professor, it's about you.'

'Me?'

'Yes, Professor, about you and someone important to you.'

Rachel? Oh, God, had something happened to her?

'Go ahead, speak. I'm listening.'

'It's about a friend of yours.' A long pause. 'Pedro,' said the voice. 'It's about Pedro.'

'Pedro,' Raphael gasped. 'Is he here in New York?'

Was it a lifetime, or a day, since Raphael had last seen Pedro? Pedro, who had disappeared behind the Iron Curtain without a trace. Pedro, who was probably in prison. Or in a Siberian labor camp.

'No, he is not in New York. I wanted you to know that I knew him, that's all.'

'And that couldn't wait until tomorrow morning?'

'Not after what I just finished reading in one of your books. Your portrait of Pedro is utterly false. Professor, let me tell you about your friend Pedro. He is totally amoral. A sadist. He made me suffer. And not just me, there were many others.'

Raphael felt the blood rushing to his face. Who was this maniac?

'Mister, who are you? How dare you call me to slander my friend?'

'You still believe in him, don't you, Professor? Well, let me tell you, you're dead wrong.'

A click. He had hung up. Raphael rubbed his eyes: had he been dreaming? To hell with asceticism. To hell with the exams. Once again, Pedro had turned up unexpectedly. Once again, Raphael was reminded of just how unpredictable he was.

Pedro, do you know that after all these years I'm still struggling to understand your role in my destiny, your attitude toward fate? It is enough for me to say your name for you to become present, and for all the years that have elapsed to fall away.

Tonight, I pay homage to you, Pedro, for you have always been at my side. I pay homage to you because your secret nourishes mine. I pay homage to you, Pedro, for you have sacrificed yourself for someone you did not even know.

Listen, all who will listen. Listen to my friend. Set him free. He is innocent. I vouch for him. Don't believe the anonymous slanderers. My friend has done no wrong. He has never sullied another man's honor. Not only is he noble and proud, he makes others noble and proud . . . Thanks to him, I have learned to bear my unbearable suffering . . .

Pedro in France: Gare de l'Est, Gare d'Austerlitz, Gare de Lyon, Gare St Lazare. Railroad stations were his kingdom. Raphael often accompanied him, either to see him off on a mission or to greet a new group of refugees. They occupied the waiting time as best they could: drinking coffee, talking, talking. Raphael remembered Pedro once telling him at the Gare d'Austerlitz, 'Back in '36, this is where we took the train for the Spanish border.' It was there, in the International Brigades, that he had acquired the name Pedro. What had his name been before? Nobody seemed to know. Raphael asked him if he had been a Communist. 'Not at all,' he responded. 'An idealist.' When he said *idealist*, his tone was derisive.

'You understand, Raphael? I left everything behind in Poland: my home, my family, my friends. In Spain, a people was fighting for its freedom. It was my duty to join their ranks. Oh, I know, it sounds a little grandiose, this desire of mine to act upon history, to influence the fate of mankind. One had to be very young and very romantic to believe in it. I was both when I fought for the great ideals of Republican Spain. Four times wounded, several citations, photographs with General Lister and even with La Pasionaria. Harrowing nights on the eve of battles, heroic projects for the world, moments of sheer ecstasy. I wanted not only to vanquish evil, but to laugh with the woman I loved . . .'

But in the game of war, Death is always the winner, and mankind the loser. Pedro returned to France, only to be interned. He escaped from Gurs, was caught in Paris, escaped again. He landed in London, moved on to Egypt, then Palestine, where he was recruited by the Haganah. Later he was assigned to the Briha . . .

'You understand, Raphael? I was alone in the world. Everybody I loved reduced to ashes. Now you are my family. You and all the others I brought out of Poland. And so my family is now quite large. I'd like it to be even larger. A new day is about to dawn, but yesterday has not been lost. I have made the memory of time my own. You have become a part of it. You will never again be alone.'

In 1946 at Le Troupeau, there was a counselor named Charlotte whom Pedro liked. She was only eighteen but so mature that the staff often asked her advice in difficult cases. She knew how to win the trust of even the most withdrawn child. Raphael too was taken with her. But she belonged to Pedro, that was clear. They had met one Shabbat evening. After services, before mealtime, the boys and girls sang and danced in the garden – Zionist folk dances, Hebrew songs of the youth movement. That particular evening, Pedro, in his typical way, was standing off to one side, observing the scene, when he noticed Charlotte, who was also standing alone.

'Come on,' he said to her, taking her by the arm.

They stayed together until the end of Shabbat. From then on, Charlotte also paid attention to Raphael, who was known to be closer to Pedro than anyone.

One day, Pedro returned from the station beaming. Raphael had never seen him like that.

'Raphael,' he shouted. 'Your brother is alive!'

Raphael's heart skipped a beat. 'Which one?' he asked.

'The one in Russia.'

Raphael didn't dare ask for details. Yoel was alive. That was enough.

'One of our agents in Warsaw contacted me. It seems he met a survivor from Rovidok whose cousin just came back from the Soviet Union. He says he and your brother were in prison together. Our networks have already been alerted. We'll find your brother and bring him out. Raphael, you have my word.'

Raphael stared at him as if he were the Messiah. Impossible to find the words to thank him. Holding back his tears, he clasped Pedro's hand. At that moment Charlotte walked in.

'What's going on?'

'We've just had word that Raphael's brother is alive,' said Pedro. 'And we are going to bring him here.'

In her excitement she hugged and kissed them both. Raphael was stunned when she took his face into her hands and kissed him on the mouth. The first kiss he had ever received from a woman, and he owed it to Pedro.

During the days and weeks that followed, Raphael was euphoric. He lived wholly in the expectation of his reunion with Yoel. Over and over again, he imagined Yoel's departure from prison, from Russia. He wondered what he looked like now. When he had left home, Raphael was still a small boy. He could barely remember him. He could see his eyes, hear his voice, but his face eluded him. Since Pedro was often away, Charlotte did her best to distract him. She took him to the cinema, told him stories about her childhood in Strasbourg, introduced him to French literature.

In April 1947, Pedro announced his departure for Berlin. That was where he was to pick up the trail leading to Yoel.

'I want to go with you,' said Raphael.

Pedro refused. Raphael insisted. Pedro wouldn't hear of it. Raphael convinced Charlotte to plead his cause, and together they tried to persuade Pedro to set aside his misgivings, which were well founded. After all, Raphael had no passport. Nor was he up to the strain of going into Germany. The arguments against were endless: Raphael was too young, too weak, and on and on.

But in the end Charlotte settled the matter. 'Just think what it will mean to Raphael's brother to have Raphael meet him there.'

Pedro gave in.

This time it was Raphael who kissed and hugged Charlotte. They would leave one week before Passover, returning in time for the first Seder. Pedro had arranged everything: a Belgian passport in good order, round-trip tickets, and two hundred American dollars in a wallet that was a present from Charlotte. It all seemed like a dream. Will I really see my brother again? wondered Raphael.

In anticipation of the journey, Raphael could neither eat nor sleep. He talked to Pedro late into the night about Yoel, his other brothers, his sisters, his parents. He told him about the old madman with the veiled eyes, and after all those months, for the first time, he spoke of his own survival.

It had been the old madman's idea to hide among the dead in the old Jewish cemetery near the river. Even as the Polish population was busy looting the ghetto, the old man and Raphael were digging a grave under cover of night. A grave like so many others, among so many others, but covered by two boards and some branches so that air could pass through.

'You're afraid of the dead, aren't you, my boy?' asked the old man.

'Yes,' whispered Raphael.

'Imagine that you are dead and you will no longer be afraid.'

Raphael tried but failed. The idea of being dead among the dead only heightened his fear.

'That's fine, that's fine,' said the old man. 'As long as you're afraid, you have proof that you're still alive.'

Raphael dared not speak the question burning his lips: And how do I know that the dead stop being afraid?

On the other hand, what was certain was that the dead do not eat. And the old man and Raphael were hungry. At night they left the grave to look for radishes and potatoes and an occasional piece of fruit, which they brought back 'home' and silently devoured.

Raphael and Pedro talked and talked; for Raphael, silence was a threat. Pedro was worried about him. He explained that silence did not necessarily mean one had forgotten. It all depended on the quality, the intensity of the silence. It all depended on the meaning you conferred on it. It all depended on Raphael.

Through the train window Raphael watched as a devastated Germany flashed by. Emaciated men and women, children in rags. Ruins, destruction everywhere. A direct result of its leaders' folly. Now the tables had turned; the victors dictated the law. With my Belgian passport, thought Raphael, I could order these people around, these same people who just yesterday had the power of life and death over thousands and thousands of human beings marked by the yellow star. What insanity, he thought. How pathetic warriors are with their absurd, ugly wars. Why must some men kill in order to feel alive? Why must some men hold others in captivity in order to feel free? There is, in what Germany has done to Europe, a mystery of a magnitude that defies comprehension.

'I'm glad you're with me after all,' said Pedro. 'It's important for you to see this country as it is now, crushed under the weight of its own hatred. We must both remember what we are seeing. *You* must remember it all, Raphael, for the day may come when you will have to speak. And on that day you will remember me and our crossing of this wretched landscape. I may be far away by then. In Palestine, perhaps. Maybe you and your brother will be there too.'

'And the dead?' asked Raphael.

'Who knows? They may already be waiting for us in Palestine. Doesn't the Talmud say that after the coming of the Messiah, the dead will rise from their graves and crawl all the way to the Holy Land?'

'Not our dead, Pedro. Our dead have no graves.'

Pedro turned to stare out the window.

'We are their graves,' he replied after a long silence.

Throughout Raphael's stay in Berlin, he was haunted by those words. I am a grave, he told himself over and over. He dreaded the moment when he would have to tell his brother Yoel that he too was a grave.

'So, Professor, have you changed your mind yet about your friend?'

That same cold voice. At midnight. Raphael had been waiting. He had the feeling he would call back. There was more to come.

'If you're telling the truth, why aren't you willing to meet me? Why are you so afraid to show your face?'

'Afraid? Not at all. But for now the telephone will do.'

'Okay, you claim to have met my friend. Can you prove it?'

'I can describe him to you.'

'That proves nothing. I describe him in my book.'

'I could tell you plenty of things that aren't in your book.'

'Like what?'

'That he disappeared in East Berlin.'

One point in the caller's favor. All Raphael had said was that Pedro was missing behind the Iron Curtain.

'What else?'

'He told me about a girl in France whose name was Charlotte.'

Obviously this fellow had met Pedro, or someone who knew him.

Raphael was determined to pin him down. 'Did he tell you what took him to East Berlin?'

'He went there to see an agent of the Briha.'

'Is that all he told you?'

'The agent had promised him information about your brother.'

'Yoel?' Raphael had let his brother's name slip out.

'Yes, Yoel. Who was in prison somewhere in Russia . . .'

Berlin, crossroads of victory. Pedro and Raphael shared a room in a requisitioned hotel. The porter was obsequious, the waiters tried too hard. The lobby was jammed with men in uniform and swarms of obliging women. All the Allies were represented: Americans, British, French, Belgian, Dutch. There were officials of the Joint, UNRRA, the Red Cross. The place was crawling with 'guides', smugglers, real traders in false documents, false traders in real documents. Everything was for sale, it was only a matter of price. Pedro offered to show Raphael the city. Raphael declined. He felt anxious, fearful. Fearful of whom? Of what? He couldn't say. Too many crimes had been conceived and implemented in this place. Raphael recoiled from touching any hand, any object, any tree that had been there *before*. No, a walk through the city did not tempt him. Stones and objects also retain the past, his friend the old madman from Rovidok had once told him. All he really wanted was to be alone, to imagine his meeting with Yoel. He'd wait for Pedro back at the hotel.

When Pedro returned, he had a young woman in UNRRA uniform in tow.

'This is Doshka,' he said. 'She is my friend. To others she is a legend.'

She extended her hand. Raphael took it. A legend? For her beauty? Unlikely, he thought. Then he caught himself. She must be beautiful inside.

'Doshka wants to know everything,' said Pedro. 'I mean everything about Yoel.'

They talked about Yoel for what seemed like hours. Raphael said whatever came to his mind. Doshka knew how to extract all useful details from his memory. To lighten the mood, she steered the conversation away from Yoel. She told of her exploits, tossing off a caustic remark here, a bawdy comment there. She got away with all of it. To his surprise, Raphael liked her. Wavy black hair, big brown eyes, tight pink sweater.

Pedro offered her vodka. She downed it Cossack-style, in one gulp. He offered her another. Again she swallowed it in a single gulp.

'What about you, little one?' she asked. 'Don't you ever drink?'

'I don't know how,' Raphael answered, blushing.

'I'll teach you.'

'Doshka,' said Pedro, pretending concern, 'lay off the boy. Unless you want him to fall in love with you.'

Doshka smiled, looking pleased with herself. I hate her, thought Raphael.

Pedro's mood seemed to change abruptly.

'Let's get back to serious matters. What about Yoel? What next?'

'Let's look at the facts,' said Doshka crisply, responding to Pedro's tone. 'This is what we know. That Yoel is alive. That he is ill. That he is in a prison hospital in Krasnograd. And that we have the means to contact him. All we need to determine is how to get him out of the hospital.'

Her analysis of the situation was quick and to the point. The odds? Fifty-fifty. In their favor? The chaos that prevailed in postwar Europe.

'Let's summarize,' said Doshka. 'Pedro, Yasha and I will travel to Krasnograd by car. Soviet officers on a mission. Our papers will be in order.'

'Fine,' said Pedro. 'We are in Krasnograd. What next?'

'Here's my plan. We go to the hospital. A physician friend provides the necessary information: topography, schedules, et cetera. We have orders from the NKVD to transport the ailing prisoner to Moscow. Yasha supplies the appropriate documentation. Once Yoel is in our hands, we're in good shape. A military car stands by, and we're on our way back to Berlin.'

'What about Raphael?' asked Pedro.

'He stays here,' said Doshka. 'The little one stays here.'

The little one, that's me, thought Raphael crossly. He protested, refused to stay behind. After all, Yoel was his brother.

'The little one will wait for us here,' she stated flatly, closing the subject.

It's hopeless, thought Raphael.

After discussing some final details, they decided to leave that very night. Doshka would return around 9 P.M. with a uniform and papers for Pedro.

'Don't worry, little one,' she said as she got up to leave.

'We'll be back in a few days. With your brother. We'll celebrate Pesach together. Either here or in Paris.'

Pedro took her downstairs, came back grinning. 'What a woman!' he said to Raphael. 'Don't you think?'

By all accounts, Doshka was a true heroine. Nothing daunted her. Not only had she saved hundreds of Jews during the war, but a number of Jewish officers had defected from Russia with her help. She was daring, defiant, resourceful. She had contacts at every level of the hierarchy. She spoke Russian, English, German, French, Romanian, and Yiddish. Her charm and wit, her easy camaraderie, endeared her to generals and corporals alike. Not to mention the intellectuals and black-marketeers.

'What a woman!' repeated Pedro, still grinning.

At precisely nine o'clock that night, she knocked at their door. The Soviet uniform suited her. She was a captain, Pedro was to be a major. The two were in excellent spirits. As they prepared to leave, Pedro opened his wallet and took out a few bills.

'Here is another three hundred dollars. That way, with what you already have, if you feel like having a good time . . .'

'Thank you, Pedro. But I won't need it. I won't be going anywhere.'

'In that case, keep it for me. That's one way of making sure I won't spend it.'

'All right,' Raphael said weakly.

Pedro held out his hand. Raphael squeezed it hard. His heart was heavy. Doshka leaned over to kiss him, but changed her mind. A handshake would do. Raphael wanted to go down to the lobby with them. Pedro said no. The door opened. The door closed. It closed on a whole chapter of his life.

He never saw Pedro again.

*

'Your friend and I crossed paths in 1948,' the stranger told Raphael the third time he called. 'We shared lodgings, if one can call them that. To be more precise, we shared a cell in the Butyrka.'

By this time, Raphael was convinced that the caller did indeed know something he didn't know about Pedro. He had to see him. He had to persuade him to show his face. Repeatedly, Raphael tried to steer the conversation back to the caller: Where was he from? How long had he been in the United States? Despite his accent, his English was good. Did he know Yiddish? Raphael tried one question. He answered in kind but soon reverted to English. Perhaps he worried about betraying himself in his mother tongue. One tended to be more careful when using acquired words.

'There were fifteen of us in the cell,' said the informer. 'When I was brought in, he was already there.'

'Already there . . . how long?'

'Quite some time. That was obvious. Longer than the others. It was he who initiated me into prison life, who told me what to do, what not to do. I admit: he gave me some good advice.'

'Then why?'

'Why do I speak ill of him?'

'As a matter of fact, why do you?'

'Because he was a rat.'

'You're crazy.'

'Believe me. He was a rat. After every interrogation, he came back smiling.'

'So what if he smiled? What does that prove?'

'There's more. After each of his interrogations, they'd come to torture one of us. Don't tell me that was coincidence. It happened every time.'

'Every time . . . how many times?'

'Enough times to convince me he was a rat.'

'Be more precise.'

'Three times. Yes, now I remember. It happened three times. First they took away Piotr Volokhov, a famous physician. Then Borokh Genchov, a carpenter from Kazan. And then Yossif Pomsh from Kiev; I don't recall what he was anymore. That's it. Three comrades. Three torture sessions. Three times.'

'Within what time period did these interrogations occur? Three sessions in three days? In a week? In a month?'

'It all happened within four or five weeks.'

Raphael exploded:

'And that's your evidence? Your basis for slandering an honorable man? You bastard, you should be ashamed of yourself!'

'Wait a minute, Professor. You're forgetting something. The only one to come back smiling was your friend Pedro.'

This time, it was Raphael who hung up.

Doshka reappeared in Raphael's room late Passover eve. Immediately he saw the disaster in her eyes. She seemed dazed. Her hair was tangled, her uniform limp. She barely greeted him before heading for the cabinet and pouring herself a tall glass of vodka. There was something desperate and childlike in the way she moved.

'Don't say anything, little one. No questions,' she said. 'Later.'

After downing her drink, she sank onto the bed, and motioned Raphael to sit down beside her.

'I don't feel like talking. I feel like doing something else, something that will keep me from talking. I feel like getting drunk, like getting lost. I feel like sleeping, like dying in my sleep.'

And I feel like shaking you, thought Raphael. Like hurling my pain, my anger, into your face. Why don't you speak, for God's sake? Why don't you tell me when I will see Pedro and Yoel again? Why don't you stop drinking and talking nonsense? But Raphael's anger dissolved in the face of her sadness. Her defeat, her resignation were total. She looked pathetic.

'What happened, Doshka?'

'Don't talk to me, little one. Don't make me talk.'

She reached over and drew him close. Her head against his chest, she whispered, 'What now? God in Heaven, what now?' She caressed his head, his throat, his face. He felt cold, he shivered and yet he was hot, he was suffocating. I can't see, thought Raphael. My head is on fire. I have never been like this with a woman. I have never before felt the touch of a woman's body. *And Pedro in all this?* And my brother? How far away they seem, how far away everything seems. I myself am not where I am but elsewhere. I myself am not who I am but another. Why is my head spinning, Doshka? What is happening to me? 'Don't talk, little one,' she whispered, holding him, 'don't make me talk.' And that was the last thing Raphael remembered, except that her face was wet with tears and that he was kissing her eyes and that they were on the bed undressed, and that through the open window they could hear the cry of a drunken soldier . . .

All night Raphael watched her as she slept. Out of uniform Doshka seemed even more childlike. She thrashed about in her sleep. Her hand kept covering her eyes as if to shield them. What was it she did not want to see? There were so many questions Raphael burned to ask but dared not, for fear of hearing the answers.

When she opened her eyes, he blurted out, 'We were all going to celebrate the Seder together . . .'

There were tears in her eyes when she answered, 'The

American chaplain . . . he's arranging a Seder. We'll be welcome, I promise you.'

'Please, Doshka. No more promises.'

She sighed. She too remembered her promises.

'You want to know? What do you want to know?'

'Where is Yoel? And where is Pedro?'

'We knew your brother was sick. We didn't know he was mad. Stark raving mad.'

Her head propped up on the pillow, she began to talk. And Raphael, lying on his back, his eyes closed, listened. Her words penetrated him, tore him apart. Strangely, her every sentence brought him closer yet took him farther away from Pedro and Yoel. She told him about the journey. Everything went smoothly. Yasha was driving. There was a document check as they left the city, another farther down the road. Yasha exchanged pleasantries with his fellow officers at the checkpoints. Things continued to go well, even in Krasnograd. To avoid registering at a hotel, they stayed with a cousin of Yasha's. That was where they were to meet the physician from the prison hospital who was to tell them the true nature of Yoel's illness. The physician knew Yoel's story: he had worked so hard at pretending to be mad that in the end he actually did go mad. That was the problem, for while the NKVD could order the release of a sick prisoner, it had no such authority over a madman. What would the NKVD do with a madman? Pedro thought up a new strategy: to have the health department request a transfer. Yasha disagreed. For that, they needed other documents that would be impossible to produce on the spot, since all his equipment was in Berlin. Doshka suggested postponing the operation by one week. Pedro refused. Once inside the hospital, they would come up with something. He had made a commitment to Raphael; he was going to keep it.

Early the next day, they set out for the hospital. To the guard they explained that they were looking for an Enemy of the State who feigned insanity. They did not know his name, only his face.

Soon a military doctor appeared to escort them to the pavilion. They made their way through various wards, pretending to scrutinize the faces of several patients before finally 'discovering' their man. What they found was a mere shell drained of all will and feeling, a body that had forgotten to die. Doshka tried to distract the military doctor so Pedro could speak to Yoel. Doshka succeeded in her task, but Pedro failed at his: Yoel did not respond. Even when Pedro mentioned Raphael's name, Yoel did not react. He continued to stare into the void.

Meanwhile, the military doctor had noticed Pedro lingering at Yoel's side. Turning back to him he said, 'I don't know who you're looking for, but I guarantee you it's not him. This patient suffers from incurable amnesia. Besides, the charges against him are very grave. So grave that General Popov himself is monitoring his case.' Sensing that all was lost, Pedro nodded and continued his inspection. Then he thanked the doctor and left. The operation had failed.

Doshka thought they should return to Berlin immediately. Pedro, still hoping for a viable plan, argued for waiting. They compromised: one more night in Krasnograd.

Pedro woke the next morning determined to go back to the hospital for one last try. 'Sometimes you have to gamble,' he said. Doshka assumed she would go along, but Pedro insisted that she remain behind. 'If anything happens, Doshka, you will have to tell Raphael.' Doshka relented, but she was uneasy. She would have much preferred to go with them to the hospital. But this was no time to argue with Pedro.

As Pedro and Yasha were leaving, they promised to be back in two hours at the latest. Otherwise they would never make it to Berlin in time for the Seder.

Two hours later they were not back. Two and a half. Three hours. They were still not back. Doshka was frantic. By this time she was sure that Pedro and Yasha had been arrested. I must go, Doshka told herself. Otherwise, I'll also be arrested. But something kept her from leaving. She remained in the apartment long enough for Yasha to return and confirm her worst fears.

A different doctor had been on duty. Suspicious, he had asked to see their special authorizations. Yasha had tried to cover their tracks: they were carrying out a covert investigation, their orders came from the top. The doctor let them proceed. Once more Pedro made his way through the wards. When he reached Yoel he stopped and whispered a few words to him. As if jolted from a long sleep, Yoel responded by shouting. Pedro begged him to lower his voice. Yoel's shouts became more insistent. 'I am not insane,' he screamed. 'I have not lost my memory, take me out of here. If you are really my brother's friend, take me out of here . . .' The staff came running from all directions. Pedro tried to disengage himself. Yoel clung to him, crying, 'Don't leave me here, don't abandon me.' A circle had formed around them. The doctor and several nurses were closing in. Yasha, who had been waiting near the exit, took in the hopelessness of the situation. Quietly, he backed out the door. He then raced down the street, jumped into the car, and headed back to Doshka.

'We've got to get out of here,' he gasped. 'Not a moment to lose. Any minute the police will be after us.'

'Where's Pedro?' asked Doshka.

'They got him. Right now, there's nothing we can do. When we get to Berlin . . . Now we can do nothing.'

Ten hours later they arrived in Berlin, exhausted, distraught, feeling like traitors. They had left Pedro, their friend, their leader, in enemy hands.

'Don't blame yourself,' said Raphael, stroking Doshka's hair. 'You did all you could. If anyone is to blame, it's me. I should never have let you go.'

'Don't talk nonsense,' said Doshka. 'Just make love to me.'

As Raphael took Doshka in his arms, his last thought was: Yoel is locked up in a madhouse, Pedro is in prison, or maybe even dead, and I am in Berlin, making love to a legend.

A lifetime later, Raphael still felt guilty.

Pedro, you were my first friend after the war. My postwar memories revolve around you: our conversations, our walks through Paris, our fateful trip to Berlin. I remember an evening at Le Troupeau when you tried to explain to me your devotion to the children who had survived:

'When a father sees his child for the first time, he can't believe that this child is his. But soon he discovers a sign, something that makes this child his own. When I look at you, the children who have come back, it is like that for me. First, I can hardly believe you're alive. Then I discover the secret sign that binds us, the secret sign of memory . . .'

Another time, as we were browsing through the bookstalls along the Seine, I told you that I often felt I lived in place of another, that I had trouble accepting that I was alive.

'That's normal,' you said. 'Like the man who sees his newborn child, you too are astonished. Astonished to have survived, to have lived all that. You open your eyes and say to yourself: Is it possible? Is this really me? This astonishment becomes the essence of your life. How diminished we would be without this capacity to let go, to abandon ourselves to the innocence of astonishment . . .'

Another time, after a concert at the Salle Pleyel, I asked you the timeless question: how man, creator of such beauty, can commit such hideous crimes.

'I know the question torments us both,' you said. 'We may never find the answer. Still, let us search for it together.'

During that period, you were sometimes critical of my moods.

'Raphael,' you said, 'the difference between us is that I invite hope and you invite despair.'

Then you stopped and smiled: 'And yet look: fate has brought us together. Isn't that reason enough to go on?'

Go on to what? For what purpose? Questions, endless questions. Why so many victims? Why so many children among the victims? Why the indifference of the Allies? And question of questions: why the silence of God? Why did I survive while my brother Ezra did not? Why did I survive instead of Ezra? Who held the pen that inscribed one person's name into the Book of Life and another's into the Book of Death?

I was right to ask these questions, you said. But then you added, 'If you try to seize the answers they will elude you. Don't be discouraged. Like the question, the answer needs freedom. But while the question never changes, the answer is ever-changing: What is important for man is to know that there is an answer. What is important for man is to feel not only the existence of an answer, but the presence of one who knows the answer. When I seek that presence I am seeking God.'

'Are you telling me you believe in God?' I asked you.

Ignoring my question, you went on:

'As I move closer to man, I move closer to God. Nothing will divert me from this path. I want you to remember this, Raphael. Should one of us disappear one day, and should we be accused of this or that, we must promise to consider whether the act as charged is true to our ideals. I know my vision of man is demanding, for it involves confronting life in order to deny death.'

'Pedro, are you telling me you believe in God?' I asked again.

You laughed, and your laughter was without malice.

'That is something you'll have to ask God,' you replied.

Pedro, my friend. I will ask God. I'll ask Him that and more.

*

'I'm telling you, Professor, your friend betrayed you.'

Raphael had become used to these midnight calls in which the stranger baited him, manipulated him into discussions. The more Raphael protested, the more abusive he became: Pedro was a Soviet collaborator. Worse, he was an *agent provocateur*, an informer, a traitor.

'Listen, mister,' Raphael told him, 'either you agree to meet me or you stop calling. Otherwise, I will call the police.'

'Are you threatening me?'

'I am.'

'That's ridiculous.'

'No, it's not. Your attempts to discredit my friend are despicable. Why do you do it?'

'For the sake of truth. For the sake of all those who were tortured because of him. You have made a saint of someone who was beneath contempt. I know. I was there. You weren't.'

The caller went on heaping insult upon insult. He called Pedro an egomaniac, an opportunist, a sadist . . .

Raphael asked himself why he put up with these hateful conversations. After all, he could have changed his telephone number, gone to the police. But something held him back. Was it masochism? he wondered. Was he trying to expiate his guilt over letting Pedro try to save Yoel? Or was it more pragmatic than that? Was he hoping to extract a clue to Pedro's whereabouts?

'Listen, mister,' Raphael said to the caller, 'if you want to blame someone, blame me or my brother Yoel. I am responsible for Pedro's going to Russia. And Yoel is responsible for his arrest. If Yoel hadn't been mad, Pedro would never have gone to prison. It's that simple. So blame me, blame my brother, but for God's sake leave Pedro out of it!'

Sometimes Raphael managed to stay calm; other times he lost his temper and screamed into the phone. How he hated this faceless man who tampered with his past. In fact, Raphael had told the caller several times that he hated him. It never seemed to faze him. Raphael suspected that he actually liked it; he seemed to want to be hated. As if that proved something.

From the first, the midnight calls made Raphael feel as though he were embroiled in a trial. Pedro was the accused and he was his defender. But Raphael was at a clear disadvantage. The prosecutor held all the aces. Not surprising, since he had set all the rules.

Still, Raphael managed to put him on the defensive: 'You have been making these accusations against Pedro. I dare you to produce someone, somewhere, to corroborate your charges.'

Silence. The caller was silent for such a long time that Raphael wondered if he was still on the line. When he spoke, his voice was surprisingly calm and ingratiating. 'I have a suggestion. Why don't you spend some time at the Mountain Clinic?'

'The Mountain Clinic? Why? There's nothing wrong with me.'

'Take my word for it. You should go there.'

'Are you suggesting that I'd find someone there to confirm your charges?'

'All I'm saying, Professor, is that a stay at the clinic will do you good . . .'

Pedro, you are in danger. More than ever before. And it's all my fault. My portrait of you made you visible. Therefore, vulnerable. You became a target.

Someone is trying to shatter my image of you, Pedro. Someone is trying to destroy you. Is he using me to hurt you, or is he using you to hurt me?

Your presence is everywhere. I constantly feel like speaking of you and to you. I am afraid and I am sad. I will not allow our friendship to be imperiled by others. Who is your accuser? Who is this man bent on hurting us? What is he trying to accomplish with his lies? I feel anger, revulsion, sorrow . . . and guilt. But, Pedro, tell me, could his lies be based on some shred of truth?

It is impossible for me to conceive of you as dishonorable. I cannot, I will not, imagine you other than who you are for me. People will tell me that I'm not objective. So what! I don't care to be objective.

I remember you taught me that one must strive to transcend worldly passions, that one must have the courage of truth. One must push one's mind when it becomes weary. One must expand one's vision to the limits of man's expectations for man.

Where are you, Pedro? If only you could stand beside me at this window. To look at this tree, this sky, to become one with them if only for a moment. When our eyes touch them, they become part of us and something infinitely precious is born.

Now let the whole world be silent. As for you, madmen, come closer. Life does have meaning, and we shall seek it together. Come closer, madmen, look deep into the eyes of a fellow madman who stands before you and smiles at you, not knowing why. All he knows is that he recognizes his fear in your madness and his own.

Why did your enemy lure me to this clinic, Pedro? What business do I have with these madmen?

The summer is coming to an end. Soon I'll pack my bag, take leave of Cain and the Messiah, of Moses and Joseph, and go home. Back to my work. Back to my students. At least that's something.

What have I learned about the plot against you, Pedro? I listened to all the patients. None is suspect. No voice resembles that of the midnight caller. No past reveals a link with you. Have these months been wasted?

I now know with greater certainty than ever that your enemy is my enemy. If only I could speak to him right now, I would unleash my contempt, my rage. I would tell him that he is nothing but a core of hate within a mass of prejudice and rancor.

I would say to him: I condemn you, you who are judging another. Because your purpose is evil. I believe in Pedro more than in myself. Pedro taught me to love mankind and celebrate its humanity despite its flaws.

If only I could understand why your enemy insists on opening old wounds. Why is truth so alien to him? I do think that he too has suffered. That is what he says, and for once I believe him. But by maligning you, Pedro, he debases his suffering.

From the first, his plan must have been to send me here so that I too would go mad. But wait a minute: a madman who knows he is mad is different. A madman who knows he is mad is a madman apart.

Confronted with such malevolence, what is one to do? To shrug it off and say 'That's life' resolves nothing. Because at this very moment, there are men everywhere suffering and inflicting suffering on others. Yes, life is deprivation, but it is also a summons.

I know, Pedro, I am delirious, swept away by a tide of madness. All these men and women who are slipping into the abyss: can they be saved? Can they be prevented from destroying themselves? Yes, one must try. First, through understanding. To say 'I understand you' means 'I want you to live.' Then, through memory. To restore their memory it must first be severed from their imaginary counterparts'.

No easy task? With a little luck, Abraham could save Abraham. Each patient tells his tale with an inspiration that carries him back to the twilight of history. And what about me? I'll be one of them soon, I may already be. I want to hide. Is that what I'm doing, Pedro? Could I be hiding behind you?

The caller tried to drive you out of my life. He failed. Does that mean I've won? Hardly. I cry into the night and the night does not answer. Never mind, I will shout and shout until I go deaf, until I go mad. Mad? Yes, I will become a madman who dreams of twilight. Did you know, Pedro, that twilight is the domain of madness?

I hear a voice from afar, a familiar voice. It tells me to walk, to keep walking, even if night is near. I am your old friend, it says, your old friend the madman. Don't you recognize me, my boy?

At his farewell dinner Raphael is seated opposite the director and next to Karen. Could he be dreaming? Is it really Karen's foot nudging his under the table? Raphael pretends not to notice. But he is perplexed. All this time she has rejected his advances, and now that he is leaving, she is flirting with him.

Raphael has been sitting there thinking how professional this conversation would sound to an outsider, and how much like gibberish it sounds to him. Neuroses. Psychoses. Affective syndromes. Once again, Raphael is struck by the abysmal level of the staff's discussions. Have you read Professor Landowski's latest diatribe against psychiatry? What, you weren't invited to the Psychiatric Conference in Honolulu? What misers they've become . . .

They linger over specific cases: the urgency of a genetic test for Adam; the Messiah's deteriorating neurochemical function; Cain's reaction to the increased lithium dosage . . . Gustavsen, the visiting Swedish authority on biochemical therapy, abruptly changes the subject. He proposes fellowships for an ethnologist from Paris and a neurologist from London. Why? Because chromosomal anomalies play a determinative role in the brain's capacity to recognize danger. Yes, Professor, says the director, but aren't you forgetting the immunological defenses? In fact, Gustavsen had forgotten all about the immunological defenses . . .

Only half listening to these exchanges, Raphael is grateful

that he has had so much contact with the patients. Otherwise, these good doctors might have pushed him over the edge. If he has to listen to their rantings much longer, they still may. Salvation comes from the far end of the table, from Joan, the pretty young intern from California. She is smiling at Raphael, displaying her perfect West Coast teeth. Joan has helped him through several rough nights. Do any of the others know? wonders Raphael. Could that be the reason for Karen's sudden interest in him?

'Professor Lipkin,' says the director, 'you have put our library in order. We are eternally grateful.'

'You are too kind.'

'Can't we persuade you to stay a little longer?'

'I'm afraid I really must go home.' He invents: 'Someone is waiting for me.'

'I wonder who,' says Joan, flashing another smile.

'I think you're afraid,' says Karen, looking straight at Raphael.

'Are you afraid?' asks Gustavsen, suddenly interested.

'I am afraid. Of invisible walls. Of the walls surrounding this clinic, surrounding its patients.'

'There are walls everywhere, my dear Professor. Even around people who are not ill. Surely you know that.'

The talk goes on around Raphael while he withdraws into himself. He already sees himself far away. With his Rachel. I don't even know where she is, he thinks. Much less what to do about her. I must get out of here. This clinic has taken its toll on me. If I don't leave now, I may never leave.

And Pedro in all this? Pedro, who sits in a prison somewhere, and for whom the walls are not abstractions.

After the meal the director asks Raphael to his office. Before they sit down, he hands Raphael an envelope with his salary. Raphael nods and puts it into his pocket.

'So?' says Benedictus. 'Now that you're leaving us, what are your conclusions?'

'I have none. Karen is right. Hospitals frighten me. Especially this one.'

'Frighten you? Why would our clinic frighten you?'

'Your patients unlocked for me a universe I didn't know, a world parallel to my own. I discovered a way of life that is alien to me, but with a logic as valid as my own. This is a troubling place. In the outside world, history is essential to progress. Here at the clinic, history is the stuff of hallucination.'

The director nods in agreement. 'Your observations are most interesting.'

As the director speaks these words, Raphael detects the barest trace of an accent. How strange that he never noticed it before. Could Benedictus be the midnight caller? Raphael stares at him, as if he were seeing him for the first time.

'Dr Benedictus,' ventures Raphael hesitantly, 'may I ask you a question?'

'Of course.'

'Where were you born?'

Benedictus scowls, peers at him from behind half-closed lids. Is there malice in his gaze?

'I don't see the relevance of such information.'

Raphael's suspicion swells like an infected gland. Yes, it is he. Benedictus is the midnight caller. Raphael is convinced of it. But why? What benefit could he possibly derive from such a game? Unless . . . unless he too is mad.

'Then let me ask you another question. Have you ever known a man, an extraordinary man, named Pedro?'

'Pedro, Pedro . . .' he says. 'Is he a Spaniard?'

'No, he is not.'

'What makes you think that I might know him?'

'Just a hunch. He's someone I lost contact with years ago.

I've been searching for him ever since, asking people everywhere.'

The director looks at Raphael inquiringly. 'And how do these people tend to respond?'

'Some are dismissive, others think I'm mad. Still others understand and offer to help me find him.'

Tensely, Raphael awaits his response. He hopes he will speak. Speak and betray himself once and for all.

'In what category do you place me?'

'The third. I hope I'm right.'

'You are, Professor. I'd like to help. If ever I meet your Pedro, I'll be sure to let you know, that's a promise.' He smiles.

Raphael nods. Surely he has been mistaken. 'In return for that promise, I'd like to tell you a story I heard as a child. Let it be my farewell story to you.

'Once upon a time, in Poland, a poor Jewish villager walked from morning till night to see the *Besht*, the Master of the Good Name, and begged him for his blessing. The man was childless and desperately wanted a son. The *Besht* blessed him, and one year later he became a father. The boy was his father's greatest joy. At three he learned to pray. At five he was reading the Bible. But soon after turning six he died. The distraught man carried his son's body all the way to the *Besht*'s house. But when he asked for the *Besht* he was told by his servant that the holy master had died four years earlier. Where is he buried? the man asked. The servant took him to the site. The man laid his son's body on the *Besht*'s grave with these words: 'Master, I asked you for a living child, not a dead child,' and he left.

'And from his grave, the *Besht* spoke to the boy: "Cry out, my child, you must cry out, while your father is still in the cemetery, before he crosses the gate. If you do, he will hear you and take you home. If you don't, he will leave and you will die again." '

The director looks puzzled. Why has Raphael told him this story? But before he has a chance to ask, Raphael gets up, shakes his hand, leaves the director's office.

He decides to take one last walk. His train is not due for a while. There is still time for another look around.

He steps out into the garden, fills his lungs with the crisp autumn air. It's getting late. The blinding colors are giving way to darkness. Across the valley, a thousand fires light up the horizon and are extinguished almost at once. All that remains visible are the dark mountains, standing out like the ramparts of a fortress. Twilight no longer seems distant. In a moment, it will envelop the earth as it has just enveloped the sky. At its approach, all creatures hold their breath, bow their heads, and put themselves at the mercy of the elements.

Raphael finds a bench, sits down. A man is sitting at the other end. Raphael tries to see his face.

Who is he, Pedro? Help me. I see only his profile. The rest of him seems embedded in the black rock jutting out into the darkening sky.

'Look,' he says. His voice is resonant and melodious, tinged with sadness. 'Day and night are in mortal combat. Since creation they have been at a stalemate. Why do they fight? They alone understand their struggle.'

He does not introduce himself. He does not have to. Now that he has spoken, I know who he is. In his presence I feel alone. Yet this solitude is not a burden. I am alone as he is alone. I am alone because he is alone.

I feel like speaking to him. I, who have been so intent on listening, now feel the need to reach into myself and beyond. I must speak to him of the dead who no longer speak, of the ghosts that haunt my sleep, of the memories that plague me. I must tell him what I have never told a soul.

But the man speaks first: 'This is not how I had imagined my creation. All these creatures that breathe because of me, what do they want? That I keep quiet, that I keep out of their lives. But when I remain silent, they reproach me. When I speak, they call me arbitrary. Those poor earthworms envy me. But why? Because I am invincible? So what? Do they think I like taking the blame for everything?'

As he speaks, I can sense his need to have me hang on his every word.

'If only they'd leave me alone. There would be help for the sick, a mother for every orphan, a home for every beggar. There would be peace everywhere, in heaven and on earth. No more bloody wars! No more massacres committed in my name! I repudiate them all.'

His words are spoken with such conviction that I allow myself to be carried by their cadence, their logic. Like Moses before me, I absorb his voice and it is that voice that speaks through mine. 'You say that you pity man. But tell me, where is your pity? How does it manifest itself? And why must it be so sparing? Since you are Almighty, why don't you replace man's baseness with goodness? And his cruel instincts with generosity?'

A cool breeze rustles the leaves. Raphael's neighbor turns up his collar.

'Who are you?' he asks impatiently. 'Who are you, mortal, to question the order of my creation? How dare you ask such momentous questions?'

I would prefer to say nothing, Pedro, and yet I hear myself speak:

'I have seen men suffer, I have seen children die. It is in their name that I speak to you. How can you justify their suffering?'

'I don't have to. Some men kill and people say it is my fault. Other men permit the killers to kill. Are you saying that too is my fault?'

'You could have prevented it all from happening.'

'Yes, I could have. Not only the massacres, but all that preceded them. I could have prevented the killer from being born, his accomplice from growing up, mankind from going astray . . . Can you tell me at what precise moment I should have intervened to keep the

children from being thrown into the flames? At the very last moment? Why not before? But when is 'before'? When the idea is conceived? When the order is transmitted? When the hunter sights his prey? Go on, answer! You are putting me on trial. Fine. But a trial involves facts and arguments, not clichés. Since you are so clever, can you tell me what I should have done, and when?'

I am dumbfounded. I don't know what to say. Surely if the man seated next to me is God, he knows my answers before I do. But if he is only a patient who thinks he is God, how can I possibly make him understand that which I myself fail to understand?

'I'm not God,' I say, forcing myself to be calm. 'I do not have a cosmic view of events. I can only speak of individual cases, tragedies that have affected me. The first victims of the ghetto: the starving children, the frightened old men. Why didn't you save my parents, my brothers and sisters, my friends? Merciful God, God of Love, where were you and where was your love when under the seal of blood and fire the killers obliterated thousands of Jewish communities?' As I speak, I feel anger and indignation pour out of me. Whether my neighbor is God or not, these are words demanding to be spoken. I have no right to hold them back.

'You hurt me,' says the patient, his head slightly bowed. 'You can't imagine how much you just hurt me.'

And, Pedro, his voice is so sad that I immediately regret my words. As I turn toward him, I think I see tears rolling down the side of his face. I tell myself: this suffering is human, not divine. Here is a madman who believes he is God, and here I am, addressing him as if he were . . .

A memory:

A Shabbat afternoon in Rovidok. Raphael was making his regular visit to the old man with the veiled eyes. The war was raging, but the Germans had not as yet occupied his little town. Still, the front was advancing and one heard the distant rumbling of cannons. The military command was distributing leaflets: WE SHALL HALT THE INVADER, REINFORCEMENTS ARE ON THE WAY. THE BRAVE POLISH ARMY WILL TEACH THE NAZIS A LESSON. The population, certainly the Jewish population, was skeptical. Experience had taught them to expect the worst. But they didn't yet know just what that meant.

Raphael's old friend the madman knew. 'This is your last visit,' he said. 'Next Saturday you won't be able to come. By then, the Germans will be here. And that will be the beginning.'

'The beginning of what?'

'The beginning of darkness,' said the old madman. 'The beginning of the end.'

Grasping Raphael's hand, he described his vision of the future: dismal barracks stretching as far as the eye can see, human creatures in rags scratching the earth for something to eat, brick chimneys spewing black smoke, and the whole place surrounded by barbed wire and guards in watch-towers.

Raphael interrupted him: 'Impossible. The German people is civilized.'

And the old madman responded:

'You are right, my boy, you are right to challenge my prophecy. It is contrary to all reason. To look into the future these days, I guess one has to be mad. But because I am, I see farther than you, farther than all of you.'

Meekly, Raphael asked him: '*And God in all this?* Tell me, would God allow it?'

And the old man answered:

'God? Did you say God?' And he burst into laughter. And his laughter frightened Raphael far more than his prophecy.

Another memory:

Raphael's brother Hayim was describing the massacre at Kolomey. The men listened in disbelief. And he watched them as they listened. Like the others, he wondered if his poor brother had lost his mind. Hayim told how the Germans ordered young Jews to dig a vast pit in the forest. And how meticulously they organized the massacre. As the men listened, they could hear the sobs of the mothers, they could see the fear of the children. Hayim told how some prayed and others remained silent. Raphael listened but he was too young to understand. He understood the words, but not the enormity of their meaning. It was as though the words detached themselves from one another and flew off in different directions. A clear blue day, the crackling of machine guns, men shooting, men dying, women watching as their children were murdered. It all seemed unreal.

After the men left, Raphael asked, 'How can this be true? How can man be so cruel?'

'Remember,' replied his father, 'once evil is unleashed, anything is possible.'

That night, curled up on his cot, Raphael could not sleep. The image of evil unleashed on mankind tormented him. Whose fault was it? Whose responsibility? Horror on this scale implicated not only man but God as well. Only God could vanquish evil, halt the massacres, end the wars. Why didn't He? Could He be on the side of the killers? Raphael rejected that notion. God on the side of evil? Unthinkable. Was He not the opposite of evil? He told himself that he would never accept the idea that God could be cruel. Man could be cruel, not God. He was convinced of it. But then, what about the killings in Kolomey? Yes, that was worse than the concept of a cruel or indifferent God.

Another memory:

Coming from Poland, Pedro's Briha convoy crossed Germany. It stopped in a DP camp, a camp for displaced persons. Pedro had seen to everything beforehand: beds, meals, showers, fresh clothes. The camp administration was at his disposal: this was not the first time he had come this way. Physically and mentally exhausted, Raphael tried to sleep but could not. Nearby, the sound of a conversation. Two men were reminiscing. Raphael found their voices soothing until he grasped what they were saying. Then, names he'd never heard before assaulted him: Sobibor, Buna, Maidanek, Treblinka. As he listened, a monstrous anguish took hold of him. He was carried off to an accursed kingdom where death is manufactured like any other commodity. He listened to the two men for hours, almost until dawn.

The following night Raphael was sitting next to Pedro in a military truck heading for the border, and he told him what he had overheard the night before. He asked Pedro whether he had been wrong to listen, since the two men had not known he was awake. Perhaps if they had known, they would have kept silent. Pedro's response: 'In our time, chance plays a more critical role than ever. These stories were given to you by chance. One day you may pass them on in your own way. To tell someone a story means to touch him, as the two men's stories touched you. Such is the mystery of dialogue. Perhaps these two men spoke only to be heard by you.'

Raphael was not reassured. On the contrary, his head was spinning with eternal questions about the Eternal One.

'Pedro,' he said, '*and what about God in all this?* One of the two men is a believer; he put on his *tephillin* this morning, I saw him with my own eyes. Tell me, Pedro, where was God while this pious Jew endured twenty-five lashes of the German's whip? Do you want to know what I really think? That very morning, God should have revealed Himself to him and said, "Wait a minute, you still say your prayers? You still believe in my kindness, my justice? My poor man, you are mad . . ." '

Pedro was silent. Raphael could not resist asking him what he was thinking. Pedro hesitated before answering, 'I'm thinking of how I admire those two men. They see words not as threats but as solace.' Raphael was stubborn: *'Pedro, and what about God in all this?'* Once again, Pedro took his time answering. 'God was never an obsession of mine but . . . now it is different. All I can say is: I too don't understand.' But Raphael would not accept that answer. He persisted: 'Do you think, as I do, that in these times one must be mad to believe in God?' When Pedro finally answered, his face was drawn. 'I can think of another explanation: What if it is God who is mad?' Raphael was shaken. He wanted to take a deep breath. He wanted to scream. But no sound left his throat.

Raphael recalls this conversation with Pedro as he sits beside the patient who takes himself for God. If God is mad, what hope is there for man? Could life be nothing more than the wink of a madman?

'You are suffering,' says the patient seated next to him, 'aren't you? I always know when someone is suffering. Even when he himself does not.'

Raphael doesn't answer. What can he say? It is not his suffering that is at issue.

The patient continues:

'There is suffering and there is suffering. Who is more odious than the man who laments a lost object in the presence of one who has lost a friend; or the man who complains of a trifle in the presence of one who is condemned to die? I am not suggesting you should not cry when you hurt. But if you cry only for yourself, your cry, in spite of its echo, will remain hollow. Without others, you would never know love. Without life, death would be meaningless. I repeat: What matters is not to cry for yourself. Cry for others. And for me too.'

These last four words seem not unlike a confession uttered against his will: What? Cry for Him too? Save Him too? Cry not only to God but for God? Could God need His creatures as much as they need Him? Raphael thinks of his master in Midrash, a scholar whose erudition encompassed all the classics. Raphael will never forget his commentaries on Ecclesiastes. According to him, this desperate book refers not to man but to the King of the Universe. 'For all my days are but sorrow!' That is not man howling, but God. 'We incessantly beseech God to take pity on us,' said his master, 'but who will take pity on Him? We must pity God, who suffers because of man, who suffers with man. We must pity God, who must witness His creation turning into a mockery. We must pity God, who cannot help but be God, who cannot help but be . . .'

The knowledge of Raphael's master was such that his disciples compared him to the Gaon of Vilna. He knew everything by heart and made the most subtle connections between texts. His influence on Raphael was profound. Raphael owes him his passion for study, and above all, his compassion for God.

He often invited Raphael to his home, where they would talk for hours. An avowed rationalist, he shunned mysticism. Still, if pressed, he would acknowledge its aesthetic value. 'Mysticism is dangerous,' he would say. 'It often confuses beauty and truth.'

This patient sitting beside me in twilight, thinks Raphael, is making me look into myself, into my past. He makes me see my dead father teaching his dead students, my dead mother shielding her dead children. Again that question, that terrible question: *And what about God in all this?*

Before God, there was God. And after God? After God there is nothing.

'You are right,' Raphael tells his neighbor. 'There are different degrees of suffering. Yours is surely deeper, more lasting. But why must it negate mine?'

'It doesn't,' says the man. 'No one can suffer in place of another. No one can live or die in place of another.'

'Not even you?'

'Not even I.'

'But isn't Pedro suffering on my behalf?'

'No. Pedro does not suffer for you. Nor, in spite of what you think, does he suffer because of you.'

Pedro, how can I help you? What should I do? Should I go to Russia, pound at the gates of the Kremlin, shout in the streets of Moscow? What good would that do? Come to think of it, it might lead me to Yoel.

'If you could see my face, you would see that I am smiling,' says the man.

'I imagine your smile. That's enough for me.'

'Tell me what you see.'

Raphael speaks to him of the power of imagination. As a child, he imagined the future. Now, he reinvents the past. His reinvented past is sheltered from disaster. The enemy never left his lair. The dead are not dead. And God still inspires faith. And Pedro is not dead or in prison. And he, Raphael, is still a child who prays and waits.

'Why did you choose this night to speak to me?' asks Raphael.

'I wanted to meet you before you left. I wanted to hear your stories,' says the other.

Raphael glances at his watch. It is late. He must leave for the station. But he doesn't move. The train will leave without him. Never mind. He is not finished here. The anonymous voice is still anonymous. He feels like Adam, who was asked by God, 'Where are you?' At least the voice of God is not anonymous. If it were, Adam-the-Madman would be right in saying that God should have destroyed Creation at the beginning, rather than allow man to destroy it in His place.

'It's late,' says Raphael.

'Yes, it's late,' comes the reply. 'So what?' For this patient it has been too late for a long time. Ever since he was committed to the Mountain Clinic.

But what about me? thinks Raphael. Nobody forced me to come here. Nobody? Well, that isn't quite true. The caller did. And what if the caller were God Himself? God his enemy? Why not? Since God is capable of everything, He's certainly capable of pursuing a solitary man who is more concerned with finding his friend than with finding God.

Raphael is petrified. He can actually feel his senses taking leave of him. Soon he will not be able to catch up with them. What am I thinking? he asks himself. That God has nothing better to do than plague me with nocturnal phone calls? What if it was all a dream, and I am still at home with Tiara and Rachel, and tomorrow I will wake up . . . No. I have to accept the facts. I am not at home. I am elsewhere. I have been exiled through the will of a stranger who wanted . . .

What did he want me to learn here? That human beings are frail? That their truths change? That there is one truth for the judges, another for the judged? That doubt is as necessary to faith as air is to fire? That there is only a fine line between innocence and guilt? Madmen frighten me, but not as much as those who push them into madness.

Should I have allowed myself to be lured into this world by my anonymous enemy? Raphael wonders. Allowed myself to be pushed to the edge of madness? Is it mad to risk whatever future I have by staying one more night?

I want to see the patient's face. But I am afraid. Afraid to see my face reflected in his. The patient sitting beside me? The other patients? Fantasies, all. Could it be that my anonymous caller too is a figment of my imagination? Could this clinic be the bewitched world of the *Klipot*, where no light penetrates? I remember myself as a child, listening to my old friend the madman talking to me of worlds inside worlds, of fire buried in ashes. Could it be that, a madman among madmen, I have never really lived the memories that crush me? Pedro, a myth? Tiara, an illusion?

The patient sitting beside Raphael is shivering. Madman of God or God of Madmen, he is alone and his solitude is a burden.

Raphael watches as the clouds shift above. He thinks of Cain, who dreams of a world in which brothers will watch over one another; of Abraham, who weeps over the fate of his doomed son; of Jeremiah, who refuses to sleep lest visions of his people's misfortunes make him weep with rage. Of Pedro, who is shrouded in silence. Of Rachel, whose mother tells her, 'Oh, you remember your father, he was always a little mad . . .'

From far away, a star appears. Uncommonly brilliant, it captures the essence of twilight.

The patient sitting beside Raphael raises his head to look at the sky. Raphael too looks and looks, but his eyes retrieve only twilight and it has a face, a face he has never forgotten. That of the old madman from Rovidok. Only his eyes, infinitely kind and wise, are veiled no more.

He just wanted a decent book to read ...

Not too much to ask, is it? It was in 1935 when Allen Lane, Managing Director of Bodley Head Publishers, stood on a platform at Exeter railway station looking for something good to read on his journey back to London. His choice was limited to popular magazines and poor-quality paperbacks – the same choice faced every day by the vast majority of readers, few of whom could afford hardbacks. Lane's disappointment and subsequent anger at the range of books generally available led him to found a company – and change the world.

'We believed in the existence in this country of a vast reading public for intelligent books at a low price, and staked everything on it'
Sir Allen Lane, 1902–1970, founder of Penguin Books

The quality paperback had arrived – and not just in bookshops. Lane was adamant that his Penguins should appear in chain stores and tobacconists, and should cost no more than a packet of cigarettes.

Reading habits (and cigarette prices) have changed since 1935, but Penguin still believes in publishing the best books for everybody to enjoy. We still believe that good design costs no more than bad design, and we still believe that quality books published passionately and responsibly make the world a better place.

So wherever you see the little bird – whether it's on a piece of prize-winning literary fiction or a celebrity autobiography, political tour de force or historical masterpiece, a serial-killer thriller, reference book, world classic or a piece of pure escapism – you can bet that it represents the very best that the genre has to offer.

Whatever you like to read – trust Penguin.